# Lost Lagoon

# Lost Lagoon

## A PACIFIC ADVENTURE

### BY ARMSTRONG SPERRY

ILLUSTRATED BY THE AUTHOR

DOUBLEDAY & COMPANY, INC.

GARDEN CITY    NEW YORK

# Contents

# Lost Lagoon

## PRELUDE

**O**FF THE NORTHERN END of the great Solomon
Island Group, the tramp *Antipodes* was steaming toward Singapore. She carried a cargo of specie
and she in a hurry. For it was December, 1914.
The South Pacific was being harried by raiders whose
headquarters were German Samoa. The *Antipodes*
mounted a three-inch gun on her fo'c'sle head and

boasted a gun crew of half-a-dozen Maoris. But neither Wilderson, her captain, nor Red Malloy, her rascally first mate, placed much faith in gun or gun crew: not when it came to matching skill with German auxiliary cruisers and U-boats.

The Pacific is a lonely ocean and the war was young. The naval power of John Bull and his allies had still to be proved, while the joined forces of Jellicoe's and Beatty's super-dreadnaughts were little more than a myth in this far corner of the world. It was every man for himself and devil take the hindmost.

About a mile to leeward of the wary *Antipodes* a long, sinister shape rose from the water. It might have been a dead whale floating to the surface. But Captain Wilderson knew that kind of fish.

"It's a sub!" he shouted. "Man the gun!"

The Maoris were in a funk. They fumbled badly. Besides, something seemed to be the matter with the three-inch gun. It jammed. And then they felt rather than heard a dull crash, a heavy thud, under their very feet. The *Antipodes* trembled—wrenched in every bolt and plate.

The U-boat submerged—disappeared from the sight of men. Mortally wounded, the *Antipodes* steamed ahead with her pumps working day and night; steamed ahead until she sank.

Only one man of the crew of eighteen returned alive to New Zealand. This man knew why the three-inch gun had jammed. He knew where the steamer lay with her cargo of specie; the bearings of the exact spot were branded into his brain. But when Red Malloy was lifted out of the battered lifeboat his memory was a blank, or so it seemed. . . . He could tell them nothing.

But that is the story.

# CHAPTER I  YOUTH SETS FORTH

D o you sell this property willingly, *m'sieu*, and in full knowledge of what you are doing?"

The French lawyer and his client, Wong Fu, were waiting for Judd Anders to speak. But the boy was silent. Through the open doorway of his bamboo house he could see the banana trees tossing like ragged banners in the southeast trade wind. Beyond the barrier reef a sailing outrigger heeled far over to a spanking breeze. Judd's heart contracted. He was remembering that his father and mother had built this house before he was born; as long ago as 1918, just after the Armistice. It was the only home the boy had ever known. And in this fateful moment it seemed to him that there was something timeless and everlasting about the bamboo house; that, like the reef and the mountains of Tahiti, it must have existed when the round earth first was molded and set spinning. Sell it? Why?

The voice of the French lawyer brought him back with a start: "*M'sieu*, do you sell this——"

"Yes, certainly!" Judd broke in, impatience edging his tone. He made a resigned gesture; it would be good to have the whole thing settled.

"*Bien*. But what is your age, *m'sieu?*"

"Seventeen."

The Frenchman shrugged deprecating shoulders. "But your signature will not be legal unless countersigned by your guardian. Have you a guardian?"

Judd smiled slightly and glanced across the room at Mata Afa. The old native—clad in *pareu* and starched white coat—sat on the floor with his back to the bamboo wall, watching the proceedings with sorrowful eyes. Good old Mata Afa. . . . Judd's guardian? Why, he had been his second father, his older brother, his devoted friend ever since the boy was born.

"Mata Afa will countersign."

The Frenchman smiled. "That will suffice." A document bristling with the red wax and blue ribbons of French legality was shoved across the table. Wong Fu straightened and smiled with inward unction. So (he was thinking) with one stroke of this boy's pen he, Wong Fu, would become owner of this fine coconut plantation of one thousand trees, and of this bamboo house which (he made mental reserve) he would immediately roof over with galvanized iron. In his belief these native thatches were good for naught but to harbor rats and lizards.

Judd looked from the Frenchman to Wong Fu. He felt sure that this sale was a wise undertaking, the only move for him to make at this time. How else could he raise money to go to America to college as his father had made him promise to do? The boy picked up the pen and scratched his name hastily at the foot of the document. There—it was done. Mata Afa, frowning laboriously, inscribed the letters of his name. The Frenchman added a blob of wax and pressed a seal into its smooth surface. Then, and not until then, the honorable Wong Fu drew from his wallet a bank draft for fifty-eight thousand francs: some two thousand dollars. Judd had never had so much money in his possession in his whole life. It would pay his passage to California, get him launched at the University, start him upon a new and strange existence. But his heart was heavy within him. He felt no personal dislike for Wong Fu, but he hated to think of the greedy little Celestial in possession of this plantation which his father had worked so hard to build. As for the Frenchman—he was the kind of colonial official in this outpost of empire who always had reminded him, somehow, of the pilot fish that swam beside the jaws of their masters, the sharks.

"Wong Fu wishes to know when he may take possession of the plantation," the Frenchman was saying.

"Tomorrow if he likes," came Judd's brief answer. "I shall be gone."

The boy and Mata Afa watched the Chinaman step into his battered Ford, while the Frenchman, nimble as a cat, sprang up beside the driver. The car rattled out of sight down the palm-lined road. The check for fifty-eight thousand francs lay on the table where Judd had dropped it. The boy turned away. It was finished. For a moment there was silence between him and the tall old native. Then Mata Afa took the boy's hand and pressed it, his black eyes looking into gray ones that were almost on a level with his own.

"It is the affair of God," Mata Afa said at last. "The waters of the rivers flow forever; old sharks die and young ones take their place; the palm tree sprouts, grows, withers. And the heart of man is forever questing. It is right that you should go. It is time."

Judd gripped the bony brown hands with both his own and could find no words. How could he leave Mata Afa and Tahiti, and this valley where he had been born? Outside the window he saw tropic birds white against the sky, trying to choose between heaven and earth; the murmur of the distant waterfall hidden within the jungle whispered its secret in his ear; on the reef the sea muttered in its sleep. And standing there with that old Polynesian in the fragrant, fertile solitude that is Tahiti, the boy knew that however much thereafter he might be submerged by the outside world—the world of machines and men and revolution and tragedy—he would never forget that he had been privileged, like the first mortal, to live close to the dark heart of this equatorial land.

He had given away the few possessions of any value which had been his father's. He would start upon this new journey as lightly laden as might be. His outrigger canoe lay drawn up on the beach like a long slim fish, suggesting that at any moment it might return to its proper element; the outrigger was now Mata Afa's. Tetua Nui, the old man's wife and Judd's foster mother, would receive the bamboo furniture and the phonograph. A few books—these for the Protestant missionary who, but a week since, had read the simple burial service over Dexter Anders, Judd's father.

The boy opened a square of red-and-white *pareu* cloth and spread it on the bed. Upon this he laid a pair of clean ducks, an extra shirt, comb, and toothbrush. He hesitated, took down from the shelf a copy of Bowditch's *Navigation*, placed it within the bundle.

"Idiot!" he muttered to himself. "What use will Bowditch be on the mainland? You're coming to anchor, Judd my lad."

But Bowditch had traveled too many miles with him in his father's trading schooner to be deserted now. The book had been his First Reader, his Iliad. . . . He grasped the corners of the *pareu* and brought them up to tie a knot. Then he thrust a stick through the knot. He grinned at Mata Afa and said, in English: "I feel like David Balfour setting forth for the House of Shaws." And the old native nodded his head and smiled in complete sympathy, though he understood not a word the boy was saying. There was one last thing to do, one thing that Judd had delayed for the final hour.

Now he climbed the hill behind the bamboo house, following the path that led along the river. It twisted through groves of magnificent *mapé* trees—the island chestnut—whose buttressed roots writhed over the ground in strange tormented shapes. In some places, half overgrown by the possessive jungle, the boy passed crumbling *maraes:* the ceremonial places of the ancients. He passed, too, deserted house-platforms all but obliterated with tangle. Once this valley had teemed with life, resounding to the boom-boom of the great drums which summoned men forth to war, to worship, to sacrifice, or to feast. Now the *maraes* and the house-platforms stood empty. In all this valley there was no sound save the rushing river. Perhaps it was this very quality of silence which most distinguished the island world from all others. No hum of insect, no cry of bird or beast, no sound of human footfall. Only an overwhelming solitude; a silence strangely intensified by the soft hiss of the waterfall, the muted rush of the river. The river was the only living thing left of the drama that had been played out in this valley centuries ago. In its rapid restless heart there was a continuity of life that reached back like a bridge flung across time. Judd found himself wondering, as he picked his way up the steep path, what life might have been like in those far-off, happy, savage days before the white man arrived with his gifts of plague and illness; those gifts which were to decimate a people whose healthy blood contained no antibodies to fight disease.

Looking upward as he climbed, the boy caught at last a glimpse of a whitewashed board church, sharp cut against the green. Behind the church the jagged peaks of the *Diadême* looked like a row of teeth in a shattered jaw. Now there came to Judd's ears a sound of singing—rich, full-throated, surging upward in one of the stirring *himenés* of the South Seas. Originally, perhaps, this tune had been "Onward, Christian Soldiers," but generations of primitive singers had set their own mark upon it. It was music caught from the sea's deep bass, the wind's high treble; resounding syllables, telling the epic of an ancient race lost within the charmed valleys of the gods: such music as Judd had heard among the first sounds of his conscious life. Now it warmed his heart with its familiar certainty.

At one side of the church a breadfruit grove gave shelter to a cemetery. Hibiscus flamed in the cool shade; the scent of *tiaré tahiti* and *frangipani* lay heavy on the air, while great golden wasps hummed above thickets of yellow *cassi*. In one corner two coral tombstones stood shoulder to shoulder, like two people standing together in an alien crowd. One stone was seventeen years old, placed there by Judd's father for the mother who had died when her son was born. Sea winds had scarred the coral limestone, fungus softened it with green; but the name, deeply graven, was clear and legible:

JUDITH ANDERS

1894–1922

BELOVED WIFE OF

DEXTER ANDERS

The second stone, new, and white as only coral can be, bore the simple legend:

DEXTER ANDERS

1897–1938

AMERICAN

Old Tetua Nui had made two *leis*, one of wild carnations, the other of *maile*. The boy placed them on the graves, then stood there for a long moment, a tight feeling in his throat. He was going away from Tahiti to a land which he had never seen: a land of gray skies, of chill winds, and searching cold. True, America was his own country—his father had never allowed him to forget that. But he had been born in this forgotten valley; the island world of the Pacific was the only world he knew, and he belonged to it. As for college—what did he care about classes and textbooks and fraternities? The sea had been his school and he had been content.

It is not easy for a man to leave his homeland behind him and to make a new life for himself in a strange world. As this thought struck Judd he sensed something of the courage that had brought his father to this Pacific island twenty years before. Dexter Anders —scarred by the battlefields of the Argonne and Château-Thierry, his lungs shattered by gas—had come to Tahiti with his bride, hoping to rebuild some measure of health and strength. Together they had made the bamboo house, planted the coconut trees, bought the trading schooner which was to be their livelihood. And when within two short years the first coral tombstone was placed upon the hill, Dexter Anders had taken his infant son on a trading trip through the Tuamotus. Mata Afa had been with them. His wife, Tetua Nui, had nourished the motherless child at her own brown breast, bringing him through childhood with her own children.

Since that time Judd had lived with the sea and schooners. Tahitians were his playmates. With his father he always spoke English, but Tahitian became his second tongue; then later in the local school, French, the official language of the island. What rich years those had been! Sailing through the islands of the Dangerous Archipelago; learning the lore of the sea, the beliefs of strange peoples. . . . Never had father and son been closer than these two. Dexter Anders had been middleweight boxing champion of the A.E.F., and teaching his sturdy son all the tricks of self-defense had been like reliving his own youth. Judd was an apt pupil. At seventeen he stood five-feet-ten, one hundred and fifty-five pounds of sinew; on the way to being as resourceful a boxer as ever his father had been. Take, for instance, that encounter a year back with José Fernandez. Fernandez—a half-caste from Hikueru—was a man of brawn and cunning. By a miracle of timing and good luck, Judd had knocked him out with a right cross to the jaw. How proud his father had been! Even the fact that Fernandez was a dangerous enemy failed to dim the luster of that victory.

The boy had learned navigation in the most practical of all ways—by sailing. He had sailed his father's schooner through the hazardous reefs of the Tuamotus when most other skippers hugged close to safe anchorage. The long, sun-gold days had been filled, too, with reading and study. And then—how swiftly a world can end. The dread influenza epidemic swept over Tahiti, leaving a thousand empty houses in its wake. Dexter Anders' shattered lungs rendered him a swift victim.

Through the open windows of the church the music swelled, soaring upward in an ecstasy of faith in God's grace and life eternal. The music quieted the boy, brought him some reassurance of rightness in a world gone topsy-turvy. Silently he turned and made his way down the hill. Tetua Nui would be at the bamboo house by this time, and friends from all the valley, gathering to wish him Godspeed and safe return. Afternoon was waning. It would be a six-mile walk to Papeete and he wanted to be there by the supper hour. Tomorrow the steamer from New Zealand would be docking—the steamer which would take him up to California, to the University, to a new life.

Judd found Tetua Nui awaiting him in the doorway.

"*E hoá!*" she called, and stood there watching him approach.

She was a woman cast in heroic mold, lineal descendant of the old chief-stock of Tahiti. There was something regal in the set of her fine head, in the very way her white Mother Hubbard swept about her bare feet. Her brown face was lined now with concern; she folded the boy against her broad bosom and led him within the house. A group of natives was sitting on the mats, all the young people whom Judd had grown up with: Night Moth and Man Who Laughs, Enemy Warrior, Ghost Girl, and Beaten To Death— a circle of friendly brown faces filled with sorrow of parting, ready for the ceremony of leave-taking. There are no abrupt Hails and Farewells in Tahiti; life moves in a pattern of ordered dignity, difficult for the impatient white man to accept or understand.

Tetua Nui seated herself on the floor in the center of a respectful circle, folding her great bulk with the ease of long practice. Mata Afa sat at her right hand while Judd sat facing them both. The boy was trying to impress this scene upon his memory, to store it up in mind and heart with the recollection of mellow voices and swift smiles. He would need to remember these things in the lonely world to the north. There had been times in the past when he had been acutely aware of these people's strangeness, aware of something in his own heritage which set him forever apart from them; their race and his were like two rivers which had started from the same source, but had drawn apart in history's childhood, to run in separate parallels and never again converge. They were the sum of a chain of racial events vastly different from his own. Yet in this moment he remembered only the kindliness, the childlike goodness in their hearts.

In a clear melodious voice Tetua Nui began to chant her genealogy—a record kept by memory in all families, since the Tahitians had no written language. Tetua Nui remembered forty generations, covering perhaps a thousand years. She named her ancestors in pairs, man and woman, in a tonal chant reserved for this ceremony alone. The names themselves were like banners flaunting the attainments of those vanished ancestors who had possessed them:

THE GOD WHO CUT OFF MOVING FLEETS

MAN OF THE FORBIDDEN PLACES

SOVEREIGN OF THE STARS AND MOON

COMMANDER OF THE SEA AND THE WINDS

TRUMPET ABOVE WITH THE GODS

RULER OF THE OCEAN TIDES

Names like these sang through Tetua Nui, carrying down the centuries the glory of a people who had been great when the Crusades were sweeping the Western world; names that had been old when Nineveh reared her grandeur to the sky.

As the long recital drew to a close Tetua Nui's voice faltered and grew still. Sorrow lay heavy on her heart. Her own children were scattered—her daughters married and living on other islands; her only son lost at sea. And now this son, Judd Anders, was going away. She rose to her feet and drew the boy toward her, tears on her cheeks.

"*Aué!*" she cried. "It seems but yesterday that you were no bigger than *that!*" Her hand indicated a foot of height. "Now—*aia!* Tetua Nui must look up to meet this boy's eyes."

Judd strained forward and kissed the brown cheek, his heart full.

"Come back to us, Aiu," the woman was saying, using the name she had given him as a child. "This is your home. Always come back."

"I will, I will!" the boy promised. And he knew that though he might range the world across, this charmed valley would always be home to him. Perhaps he was a fool to be leaving it. Who knew what lay in wait for him outside? But there was the promise given to his father and he must go. Some day he would come back, and Tetua Nui would be there, and Mata Afa, and Ghost Girl, and all the others. . . . Nothing ever changed in the island world: there was always the sea, the palms, and the sunlight.

Night Moth was singing, and Man Who Laughs chimed in—poignant words that carried a weight of loss:

> *"Ua rari au tino*
> *I te aré miti ra;*
> *I te haamanao raa e,*
> *Ia oe, tau here!*

> *"My body is wet*
> *With the sea's salt spray.*
> *Heavy is my heart*
> *With this parting."*

Judd picked up the bamboo stick with its *pareu* bundle, swung it over his shoulder. A flutter of paper caught his eye: Wong Fu's check. With a wry smile the boy thrust it into his pocket. Then, vaulting lightly over the rail, he started briskly down the coral road. The moving shadows of the palms had the size and shape of Gargantuan spiders; the sea shone through the trees, as blue as a sapphire's heart. Before the bend in the road shut out the bamboo house, Judd looked back. He waved once, then set his face resolutely toward the east. But long after the house had vanished from sight, the voices of Night Moth and Man Who Laughs echoed in his ears:

> "*Ua rari au tino*
> *I te aré miti ra . . .*"

## CHAPTER II   ADVENTURE IN STRANGE GUISE

J UDD HELD STEADILY along the Broom Road, his bundle swinging at the end of his stick. As the road twisted through a growth of mangoes and algarobas it never strayed far from sight or sound of the sea.

The first stars appeared, close and near at hand. Grass houses, looking more than ever like haystacks

23

in the deepening dusk, clustered under the palms where laughter mingled with the music of guitars. There were fishermen returning from the reef with the day's catch weighting their outriggers. The smoke of the cook-fires rose lazily in the quiet air. It was the hour when all men are at peace with themselves and their world. The scent of roasting breadfruit came to Judd's nostrils, making him aware of his own hunger. From every threshold he heard the inevitable Tahitian greeting: "*Haere mai tamaa!* Come and eat!" That greeting was the "Hello, Stranger" of Polynesia, telling its own tale of native hospitality. Across the bay the island of Moorea—the Eimeo of the ancients— floated on a wine-colored sea.

As Judd drew into Papeete his pace quickened. The Rue du Quai ran along the water front, where grimy pearling schooners tied up to the sea wall with their noses pointed toward the open sea—eager to be off. Chinese merchants lurked in the doorways of their shops like patient spiders sitting before their webs. Groups of flower-crowned *vahinés* wandered arm in arm down the streets, filling the dusk with their tinkling laughter. Dexter Anders always had said that Papeete was like a scene from comic opera, with its government officials resplendent in gold braid driving to the *Cercle Bougainville* for their evening's *apéritif*, while beach combers in mildewed rags sprawled on the benches under the coconut palms, like derelict ships come to final anchor.

A rickety carriage lurched down the street and the boy paused to call a greeting to its occupant. Old Marau, the last Queen of Tahiti, had been a friend of his parents. Her fine old face beamed as she leaned far out of the carriage to acknowledge Judd's salutation with a friendly wave of her hand and a cry of "*E hoá!*"

The kerosene flares of the hokey-pokey wagons disclosed an assortment of tempting foods that brought the boy back to a world of reality and healthy hunger. He made his way forthwith toward Sing Fat's restaurant.

In after years that decision—taken now without conscious thought—was to return to him; and he was to marvel at the strange and devious ways of Chance. For he might have elected to eat at the *Mariposa* or the *Diadême;* but if he had so chosen, the entire course of his life would have flowed into another channel and this story would never have been told.

All roads in Tahiti lead to Sing Fat's. It is famous throughout the length and breadth of the Pacific. It is a two-story frame building whose lower floor is a shop where a man may buy anything from a bunch of bananas to a whaleboat. Bolts of gayly colored silks and calicoes lie on shelves along the walls to tempt the Tahitian *vahinés* who love such fine things. There are knives and accordions and fishing tackle for the men. Bananas swing in ripe festoons from the rafters. The upper floor is a restaurant, and in all the islands of the Pacific there is no Chinese food better than Sing Fat's.

Accordions were wheezing out on the balcony as Judd climbed the sagging stairs and paused in the doorway. Across one end of the long room he saw counters laden with steaming dishes—unimaginable things of infinite variety: bird's-nest soup; *bêche de mer* and turtles' eggs; shellfish and sharks' fins; squid and pork; strange sauces to whet the appetite. And all manner of people were gathered here to eat: pearl traders, plantation owners, natives, sailors from visiting ships—as motley a lot as could well be imagined. Sing Fat hovered over his guests like a croupier with human pawns. It was whispered that a knife lay always close to his lean ribs; more than one man had seen the flash of its arc; more than one had felt its swift cold stab. . . .

At a table for three against the wall Judd saw a young man sitting alone. A thin, serious young man whose horn-rimmed spectacles were directed upon the pages of a book. Judd crossed over and dropped into one of the vacant chairs at his table. The thin young man did not look up, so absorbed was he in his reading. The book was a big one, thick and black, with the title stamped in gold on its front cover. Judd tried to puzzle out the title, upside down as it was. At last he deciphered it: *Polynesian Migrations*. In spite of himself the boy smiled. What manner of fellow could this be, choosing the din and hubbub of Sing Fat's restaurant as a place to read a tome on ethnology?

Judd ordered his favorite dish of pork and bamboo shoots, then settled back, letting his eye rove over the crowd.

The young man opposite lowered his book suddenly. Behind the horn-rimmed spectacles his pale-blue eyes seemed to make an effort to focus themselves upon a world of reality. He couldn't have been more than twenty-four or -five, but there was an air of solemnity about him that, oddly enough, made him seem much younger than that: like a small boy acting out a part. He was slim to thinness and the hollows in his cheek bones accented the bony structure of his face. His nondescript hair fell limply into his eyes; his mouth was wide and generous and inclined to laughter. When he spoke his voice was thin but pleasantly American. "Say, I didn't know I had company," he smiled.

There was friendliness in the blue eyes that were as open and unguarded as a child's.

Judd smiled back and said, "I didn't want to interrupt you." He had known few Americans of his own age and so there was a certain diffidence in his manner. He wasn't quite certain how to talk to this fellow. Probably fitting into American university life would be harder than he had realized.

But the young stranger enjoyed an ease that put diffidence to rout. "It'd be a good thing if more people did interrupt me," he answered ruefully. "I think I've read every book in the world! They used to kid me at college and say that I was so busy reading about life that I'd never have a chance to live it."

"Have you been here long?" Judd asked.

"Two weeks. I came down on the last steamer from the States. My name's Henderson—Ken Henderson. What's yours?"

"Judd Anders."

They gripped hands across the table. And there was something so altogether likable in this Ken Henderson that Judd's heart kindled with the certainty that he had found a friend. An American. Someone nearly his own age. If there were more fellows like Ken Henderson on the mainland the University might not be so bad! The thought struck Judd with a sense of surprise. Perhaps, growing up as he had among Polynesians, he'd been lonely for his own kind. Perhaps his father had realized this in his insistence upon a university degree. Funny he'd never thought of it that way before.

"Do you live in Tahiti?" Ken Henderson was asking. "You're almost as brown as a Polynesian."

"Yes. That is—I always have. I'm sailing for the mainland tomorrow."

"Do you mean to say you've lived on this island all your life?" Behind the spectacles the blue eyes grew round with astonishment.

"Why, yes," Judd answered. "Is that so strange?"

"It seems so to me. I'd never been out of Chicago until I came here. I'm supposed to be an ethnologist, here on a fellowship; written a couple of monographs on Polynesians, in fact. Thought I'd better come down here to see what they looked like in their native habitat before I wrote any more. Say, I wish you were staying! Do you have to leave tomorrow? You could help me a lot with my work, especially if you know a few words of the language."

A few words of the language. Judd smiled and shook his head regretfully. "I'd like nothing better than to stay and help you, but I've got to go up to the University. I'm not hankering after it, but I promised my dad I'd get something into my head besides navigation and pearl diving."

"Pearl diving!" the other breathed, his eyes shining.

A bowl of steaming food was set down before Judd, and he looked up with a word of thanks for the flower-crowned *vahiné* who brought it. "*Ia ora na*, American," the girl greeted him. "They say you are going away."

"Yes—how did you know?"

"Sing Fat has told it."

The boy laughed. "I might have guessed. Sing Fat knows all things. What else did he tell you?"

"That you sold your land for fifty-eight thousand francs."

"Another bull's-eye."

"*Aué*, we shall miss you, American." The girl's smile was wide and friendly; her teeth flashed white against the rich gold of her skin.

"I'll miss Tahiti, too. Listen—they're playing 'Te Faarui.' Sing it for us."

From the balcony came the sound of guitars and accordions thumping out the rollicking tune. The girl laughed and threw back her head:

"*Te faarui nei au*
*I tau aia e.*
*I te haamanao raa e,*
*Ia oe, tau here!*"

Through all the gay verses she sang, while the spectators banged the rhythm on the tables with their fists, stamped their feet to the lilt of it, shouted the refrain. Ken Henderson's eyes widened behind their spectacles. He leaned forward, gripping his book in both hands. He had never suspected that Tahiti was as mad, as foolish as this! Surely nowhere else in the world was there a place so absurd! Why, anything might happen here. A man could rub elbows with adventure in a hundred strange guises. This—why, this was life! Perhaps they'd been right in college— he'd been too busy reading about life to live it.

As the song ended, a tall man in white linen entered the doorway: an immaculate figure, poised, alert, and wary. The man paused for a second to let his eyes range among the tables. Judd and Ken Henderson found themselves studying him with more than ordinary interest. The two boys could not have guessed in that moment that here was one of the strange guises which adventure might take; that this man was to change the course of their lives. . . . They saw only that he was dressed with casual elegance and that he appeared to be searching for someone. The man's eyes narrowed as they fell upon Judd and his companion, and forthwith he made his way across the crowded room to their table.

"Do you mind if I sit here?"

A hint of accent shadowed his speech. Swedish, perhaps. Or perhaps not. . . . Illusive and hard to place.

Judd knew all the island planters by sight and this

AXEL BERGSTROM

man was a stranger to him. Where could he have hailed from? There was no steamer in port. Without waiting for the boys' response the man seated himself, extracted a cigarette from a tortoise-shell case, ordered a cointreau, and introduced himself.

"My name's Bergstrom," he said affably. "Axel Bergstrom, owner of the brig *Island Queen*."

So he was a Swede, was he? The man's eyes shifted slightly before the boys' steady gaze. It was Ken Henderson who filled the pause. "My name's Henderson," he offered. "This is my friend Judd Anders. Where did you drop from?"

The newcomer flashed a smile that kindled an answering warmth in his eyes. His teeth were as white as scraped bone. "Just dropped anchor here this evening," he said pleasantly. "Made a record passage from Strong's Island. Twenty-one days with a cross-wind."

Now he had caught Judd's interest. "Strong's Island?" the boy demanded. "You mean Kusaie, in the Carolines?"

"If you prefer its native name—yes."

"That *is* good time. No auxiliary, of course?"

"Nothing but canvas," came the man's answer. "I believe that sailing ships were meant to sail. I put in here to get a new skipper." His appraising eyes took in Judd's well-set frame and he said, "You're no fore-mast hand!"

The boy laughed shortly. He remembered the thousands of miles he had sailed his father's schooner, navigating the Low Islands in the teeth of all weather, plotting his course by the sun and the stars, by the feel of the wind on his cheek. He answered: "No, I'm not a foremast hand."

"You have a mate's certificate?"

"I've never needed one."

"What was your last ship?" There was an edge of insistence in Axel Bergstrom's tone.

Judd felt a rising resentment, for no reason that he could fathom. "I'm not a professional sailor," he answered shortly.

"No offense meant, my boy. You look like a deep-sea sailor. I need one on the *Island Queen*. That's all."

"Thanks," Judd began, "but I——"

"Say! Would I do?" Ken Henderson leaned across the table excitedly, his eyes bright with expectancy. The volume on Polynesian migrations slid to the floor with a bump and lay unheeded. There was an eagerness about him that touched Judd in some unaccountable way.

Bergstrom surveyed the young man with a faintly derisive smile.

"I—I know I don't look like a deep-sea sailor," Ken Henderson hurried on. "And I don't know anything about navigation. But if it's in a book I can learn it! I've got a Ph.D. and a——"

"Hardly qualifications in my business, young man," Bergstrom replied acidly.

"Oh, say, Judd," cried the other impetuously, turning to his new friend and grasping him by the arm, "why don't you tell him you'll sign up if he'll take me on, too? It's a chance to study ethnology at first hand. Go ahead, be a sport!"

"But I'm going up to the mainland tomorrow," Judd protested. "I'd like nothing better, Ken, but——" He broke off and turned toward Bergstrom. "Where are you bound, anyway?"

The man's pause was almost imperceptible; then he filled it quickly. "The South Pacific."

Judd snorted. "But you're there now!"

A flush tinged the Swede's cheek bones. "Far south of here, young man," he amended. "Would you be interested enough in a special venture to ship aboard the *Island Queen?*"

"Tell him yes," urged Ken.

The thought of adventure sang in Judd's veins but he stifled it with an effort. Yet in the very moment of refusing, his voice died in his throat. A sudden, un-natural hush in the noisy room had communicated itself to him. Or perhaps it was that in this second Fate touched him with a chill finger. Adventure in strange guise. . . . Involuntarily Judd looked toward the door. His breath quickened.

Framed in the opening stood José Fernandez: the half-caste from Hikueru. The man Judd had knocked out once, a century ago. . . . Across the room Fernandez' eyes met Judd's. The boy felt a quick tensing of his muscles. The half-caste lounged insolently in the doorway with a breadth of massive shoulder; muscles rippled beneath his tawny skin; a gold earring clipped one ear.

Seeing him now, Judd marveled at the stroke of luck that had enabled him to triumph over this Goliath that day on the beach. But what ill chance had caused him to make such a formidable enemy? Fernandez' cronies hovered at their master's elbow: South Pacific rogues and scamps—the sweepings of the Seven Seas.

In a charged silence Fernandez moved across the room straight toward Judd. The boy pushed back his chair. Ken Henderson rose also, looking startled and bewildered. The crowd strained forward. The story of that encounter on the beach at Hikueru had traveled. This was a moment that had long been expected.

Bergstrom gripped Judd's arm with tense fingers. "Careful, my friend," he warned. "I'd get out of here if I were you."

It was good advice and the boy knew it. There was a time to face danger and a time to flee from it. Well —he'd run. He swung toward the doorway at his back, where a flight of stairs led down to the street.

"*Coward!*"

Fernandez hurled the word like a missile. Judd stiffened and whirled about.

Now they were face to face. Judd looked back eye for eye into his enemy's dark countenance. What he saw would have quaked a stouter heart. The man's thick lips folded back from his teeth. This boy confronting him was inches shorter than he, pounds lighter; this boy who once had tricked him with a cunning blow, made him a laughingstock before his men. He advanced a step, his eyes red flares of hate. Judd's right fist swung to catch him in the mouth.

Fernandez stopped. Then with a curse he lunged, swinging wildly. He knew naught of fighting save to batter down his enemy with blows of his flailing fists.

In a clinch Judd would stand no chance. No one present would lift a hand to interfere. The boy felt the blood coursing like fire through his veins. His body, lean and fit, obeyed some spring of his inner consciousness. He feinted and side-stepped. The eyes of the spectators were trained upon him, speculating. . . . They saw that he was only a youth, but whipstrong, with a potentiality for speed. In Fernandez they saw a savage, slow but infinitely dangerous. And he was their kind. They guffawed at his jokes and he paid for their liquor. They knew where their bread was buttered.

"Eat 'im up, Fernandez!" yelled an encouraging voice, setting the temper of the crowd.

"Lay into him, José!"

"Flatten 'im out, big boy!"

Ken's shout, high-pitched, rose above the others: "Tear into him, Judd!"

Pandemonium broke loose. The floor sagged under the stamp of feet. Fernandez' men ranged behind their master. One of them smashed the center hanging lantern. Gloom rushed in. Shouts and yells tore the air.

Fernandez rushed. Falling back, Judd ducked and side-stepped. Then, seeing an opening, he drove a savage right for the jaw. He missed. His feet were knocked from under him. The floor rose with a crash. Up went a howl from the mob. The boy's head spun. He struggled to his knees. That instant Fernandez was upon him. Things were happening in seconds. Steel fingers reached for his throat. The column of air to his lungs snapped off. His eyes bulged in his head. His senses swam.

Blindly he gripped the man's knees, threw his weight against them, yanked with every ounce of ebbing strength. The yellow fingers slipped, loosed their hold. Air poured into the boy's lungs. The mob watched, breathless, as the two bodies writhed and twisted. In a flash of desperation Judd swung for the man's left eye: a blow that jarred him to the shoulder. With a yell of pain Fernandez flung up one hand to his eye. Here was Judd's chance. The boy broke loose, stumbled back against a table. Strength almost gone; breath tearing his throat in gasps. He threw out a hand to steady himself. His fingers closed about the back of a chair.

Fernandez whipped a knife from his belt. He lunged forward. Instinctively the boy acted. He lifted the chair and swung it downward. It crashed upon the half-caste's skull. The man staggered, fell backward, lay still.

For a split second the crowd was stunned to silence. Their idol lay breathing heavily on the floor. Judd dashed his hand across his eyes. He felt weak and sick.

The mob roused to life. "Come on, fellers! After 'im! Get 'im!" They surged forward in a wave of menace.

"This way!" shouted Ken Henderson in Judd's ear, gripping his friend by one arm. Bergstrom seized him by the other. A door opened somewhere at their backs.

"Quick, American!" It was the *vahiné*.

The boy, half dragged, stumbled down a narrow stairway to the street. He could hear the yells of the pursuers at his heels, shoving, clattering down the stairs.

He ran for the water front, Bergstrom and Ken but

a pace or two behind. An offshore breeze was blowing. It struck them like a cool hand. Past the shuttered Chinese shops they fled, through the dark streets. Dogs barked at them. Windows opened here and there, inquisitive heads thrust out into the night. Judd and his companions gained a block, turned a corner and drew up breathless at the sea wall. A dinghy was moored at the quay. They fell into it. Judd reached frantically for the oars as the first of the pack hove into sight. Out in the harbor the dim form of the *Island Queen*, Bergstrom's brig, lay tugging at her anchor chain.

"Pull!" came the Swede's hoarse shout. "Pull for your life!"

Some of the men had leaped into the water, swimming after the escaping dinghy. Their yells bridged the darkness. Judd strained at the oars. The dinghy bounced over the waves. Then it was alongside the brig. The three hauled themselves aboard, dropped on deck. The masts loomed black against the starry sky. Shadowy figures of the crew emerged out of darkness.

As the brig's forefoot came over her anchor, Judd —unconsciously taking command—shouted an order to the stupefied sailors:

"Up anchor!"

The men leaped to obey. A gust of wind canted the

ship's bows away from shore. In a second her anchor was atrip. Fore and main tops'ls filled to the breeze, bellied out. The *Island Queen* wore round and pointed her nose to the open sea. She gathered way. Through the passage in the reef she tore, white wings of spray leaping aft from the cutwater. Out into the mystery of the wide Pacific, toward the outer darkness and the unknown. . . .

Looking back, Judd found that Tahiti had been swallowed up in the night.

## CHAPTER III   MYSTERY SHIP

With midnight the *Island Queen*, quivering in
every timber, fled like a deer with the hounds
at her heels. Spray leaped high over her weather bows.
The whine of strained cordage hummed like plucked
wire above the song of the wind.

Judd Anders stood beside the helmsman, relying
for his control of the ship upon that sixth sense which

belongs to those who have been cradled by the sea. Axel Bergstrom had disappeared below, satisfied apparently that Judd was capable of handling the brig. Ken Henderson, violently seasick at the brig's first pitch and roll, had taken himself off in misery to a cabin amidships.

Judd was alone. Standing there in the darkness with the tumult of black waters round about him, a sense of isolation pressed down upon him like a hand. The stress of the past few hours was bringing its reaction. He felt numb and cold. It had all happened so quickly, it seemed so unreal, that Judd found himself wondering who he was, how all this had come about, what he should do about it, and whether anyone ever knew for certain why and by what means his affairs were shaped for him. He thought of his father. . . . What would Dexter Anders have said about this situation? How would he have acted in like circumstances? The boy wished that he knew. If only Mata Afa were here, with his sure strength and quiet wisdom. How far off already Tahiti seemed, and the University.

Ordinarily nothing could have appealed to Judd more than just such a wild adventure as this. But in Axel Bergstrom he had sensed something hidden, almost sinister, that left him with no relish for this situation. He felt as if he were swimming against the current which sweeps around the shoulder of Puna-ruu, swimming strongly, yet all the time being carried farther and farther out to sea.

Someone touched his arm. He started, and turned to find a native sailor at his side: a Samoan by his accent, Judd guessed, yet the youth was addressing him in Tahitian. And something in those familiar syllables warmed the boy's heart.

"What's your name?" he asked.

"Matu," the Samoan replied. He appeared to be about Judd's own age, a slim young Polynesian, barefooted on the wet deck, his canvas ducks rolled up above his knees. The light from the binnacle showed an open, earnest face, a shock of curly black hair, and spray glistening on his bronze skin. There was something so honest, so familiar about him that Judd's spirits gave an upward lift.

The native was saying, "Bergstrom—he wants to see you."

As Judd turned to go, the youth caught his arm in a strong grip. "I have heard what happened," he whispered. "I, Matu, am your friend."

Judd gripped the brown hand with swift pressure and silent thanks. A turn of the wheel of chance had taken events out of his hands. He had been catapulted into a strange adventure whose end was shrouded in obscurity. Somehow he was certain that he would need friends aboard this mystery ship; the pressure of Matu's hand, the sound of his Polynesian voice,

TOR JANSEN

warmed Judd's heart. He turned and made his way below.

"Sit down, Judd," Axel Bergstrom said pleasantly as the boy paused in the doorway.

There was a second man, a white man, seated in the shadows beside Bergstrom. Judd knew a feeling of surprise. Somehow it had not occurred to him that Bergstrom might have a partner aboard. The Swede introduced the stranger with a wave of his hand: "My friend and partner, Tor Jansen."

Tor Jansen acknowledged Judd's nod with a forward jerk of his head. The boy saw a grotesque figure: small, wiry, with large ears like a bat's and eyes that glittered with a strange brightness. The man uttered no sound. In his watchful immobility there was something deeply malign. It was not until later Judd realized that Tor Jansen was mute; locked within a prison of watchful silence. There was something preternaturally alert in that silence, as if in hearing alone the man concentrated two senses. He seemed neither young nor old, and his eyes held an unwavering scrutiny, impersonal yet profoundly disturbing. He was dressed in grimy ducks and a dirty cotton shirt with collar agape, disclosing a pulse beating in the thin throat. He was, in every outward particular, the opposite of his immaculate companion. Judd threw him a quick glance and looked away, an obscure apprehension communicating itself to him. . . .

Bergstrom indicated a chair on the opposite side of the felt-covered table. The boy sat down gingerly, unconsciously poised for flight. "Cigarette?" Judd shook his head. The Swede took one, tapped it on his nail in silent contemplation. Tor Jansen remained immobile, life only in his strange eyes. And thus the three sat for what seemed to Judd an interminable time. At length Bergstrom broke the stillness.

"It's a lucky thing there was a wind in that harbor," he murmured, watching the boy from under lowered lids. "That mob might have taken it into their heads to swim after us. At close quarters even a pack of rats can be nasty."

The boy shifted his weight but made no response. He was sensible of a vague distrust of this man and his strange companion.

"I think," Bergstrom was saying, "you should be exceedingly grateful to me for getting you out of such a jam." The man leaned forward, stretching his arms full length across the table. A decanter and some glasses shivered with his movement. The kerosene lamp swinging in its gimbals illumined the area around the table and brought out in sharp relief Bergstrom's thin, cold features. Tor Jansen sat just out of reach of its glow, half lost in shadow. The rest of the cabin was dark. Outside the porthole black seas banged unceasingly against the glass, to run in drops of amber down the pane. The whine of timber, the creak of blocks, the drumming of the reef points against the outer darkness filled Judd with a profound unease. At that moment he would have joyously welcomed sight of Ken Henderson with his horn-rimmed spectacles and his owlish air; he would have welcomed any familiar face or reassuring voice. Judd Anders was not overly imaginative nor easily thrown off balance by the unexpected, but tonight's experience had shaken him, and in these two men who confronted him across the green-covered table there was more than a suggestion of mystery. Who were they? Where did this ship come from? Whither was she bound? Unconsciously the boy found himself flexing his muscles, as if the menace that hung over him actually were physical. With a start he realized that Bergstrom had begun to speak; the man's tone was so low that it seemed to blend with the ship sounds, with the dark chorus of the night.

"The affair at Sing Fat's simplified matters for me," the Swede was saying. "I must confess, my boy, that I was not wholly altruistic in getting you out of that jam. There was no obligation on my part not to desert you. But I didn't . . ."

Judd stiffened. "What are you driving at?" he demanded shortly.

"It's simple. I need a new skipper. You appear to fill the bill. Karl Kassel, your predecessor, died of blackwater fever." Bergstrom filled his glass then leaned forward, and his eyes fixed the boy with intensity. He cleared his throat and went on. "The story I am about to tell you may sound fantastic, young man. You may disbelieve it if you choose. No matter. My reasons for taking you into my confidence will be clear in a moment. Would you care to hear?"

"Of—of course!" Judd's hands felt cold. He held Bergstrom's eyes by an effort of will.

"Then here's the way of it." The man drew a deep breath, exhaled a ring of smoke, and began. "Kassel was an old friend of mine in Australia. We bought this brig together to run her through Melanesia for trade and labor-recruiting. I'm not a navigator myself—haven't the knack or knowledge for it. And Jansen here doesn't know a sheet from a boom. But Kassel could sail a ship to the end of the world and back. And he was a fine friend. His death has been a great blow." The man paused, apparently moved. "He died just as we sighted Tahiti. I gave him a sailor's burial at sea, as he desired. When I sailed into the harbor tonight I was at rope's end. Where could I find another skipper—one that I could trust?"

"How do you know that you can trust me?" Judd managed.

Bergstrom smiled—a smile tinged with irony and the bitterest wisdom. "I know men. I can see through whatever front they put up: right through to the bottom of their wretched souls. I have no illusions. I do not cherish absurdities. But I know that you can be trusted."

Judd sat silent, unable to find words to meet this situation, his mind confused and groping in the dark.

"To continue," Bergstrom was saying, "Kassel claimed to know the existence and position of a sunken tramp with a cargo of specie: the Germans got her during the first year of the war. After she was torpedoed she steamed ahead with pumps working day and night, for over three hundred miles. Finally she sank in the lagoon of an uncharted island, an atoll. I admit I was skeptical when I heard the tale, for I'd listened to too many yarns of buried treasure. But Kassel had a map which carried conviction."

"Where did he get it?" Judd demanded.

"That is beside the point."

"Do you mean," the boy asked incredulously, "this uncharted atoll had never been discovered until the steamer stumbled on it?"

"Not exactly," came the Swede's reply. "A French surveying vessel—the *St. Etienne*—was supposed to have prospected the lagoon in 1888, but failing to find any shell had given it up as a bad job. The ocean for hundreds of miles in that vicinity is a network of submerged reefs, so ships have always given it a wide berth. The atoll lies in the very heart of this devilish region. It has no drinking water, only one small passage into the lagoon, and no inhabitants. There are many such bits of land in the South Pacific, as you know."

That was true enough, Judd acknowledged.

"It was only by the grace of God that the steamer reached the atoll before she sank, or her cargo would have been lost forever. The men had a chance to get themselves organized for the long trip back to New Zealand in open boats. They spent a month on the atoll before they made their getaway. They were in two lifeboats, nine men to a boat. One boat put in for water at the New Hebrides and all her men were killed by the savages. The other boat was blown far from her course. The men died one at a time of starvation, then of thirst. When at last New Zealand was sighted only one man lived to be carried ashore."

"Didn't the Colonial Government send out a salvage expedition to this atoll?"

The Swede shook his head and a slow smile crept over his face. "No."

"Why not?"

"Because that one man's mind was an utter blank, or so it seemed. . . . He could tell them nothing. The *Antipodes* and her cargo of gold had vanished." Bergstrom's voice dropped into the dark silence.

Tor Jansen sat motionless in the shadows, life only in the glitter of his eyes and in the sense of secret energy which he suggested. Judd found himself waiting with each nerve tuned—waiting for he knew not what.

"Kassel and I were convinced that this island existed," Bergstrom was saying. "We bought the *Island Queen* and decided to take Tor Jansen in with us. He's an expert diver, but he'd fallen on hard luck and lost all his gear. Buying this brig cleaned us out and we had no money for diving equipment."

"But the gold," Judd suggested quietly, "belonged to the Colonial Government."

"Gold belongs to the man who finds it, my son," the Swede reminded him with a slow smile. "And now observe how beneficent a part Lady Luck plays in the lives of men! What happened? Why, Kassel got a letter from Red Malloy—hadn't heard from him since the war. Malloy was first mate on the *Antipodes* when she was sunk. He'd been living in the Solomons ever since the Armistice and doing pretty well blackbirding. I've never met Malloy myself, but Kassel swore that he could be depended upon. And as he owned a couple of diving outfits he was the man for us. Then fate stepped in. Kassel came down with black-water fever. I did everything possible for him but he was doomed and he knew it." Bergstrom's voice had sunk to a monotone. Something in its very inexpressiveness rasped the boy's nerves as if with a file's edge.

Tor Jansen stirred for the first time, leaned forward into the circle of shifting light. His skin seemed yellow as aged parchment, tight-drawn across his skull; his lips opened slightly but no sound issued forth. Some wordless message seemed to pass between this man and his companion; it was as if they used a language of telepathic silence secret to them alone. Bergstrom inclined his head in answer to what appeared to be an unspoken question. Judd watched them, fascinated. With a furtive movement Tor Jansen reached forward and opened a drawer in the table. He withdrew a tightly rolled scroll of paper. Slipping off a rubber band he spread out the paper on the table top while Bergstrom thumb-tacked the corners into place with fingers that trembled. Involuntarily Judd leaned forward. He saw a scaled map of an atoll: an atoll that appeared to be a ring of five islets strung together on a thread of reef. In one corner, blurred but still distinct, was the date December 1914, and the words were traced:

VANA VANA OR LOST LAGOON

It was not different in any particular from a hundred other maps that Judd had seen; yet he found himself looking at this one with a sort of expectancy and wonder, as a man might look upon a nugget wrested out of virgin soil. Here was no ordinary map scaled by a competent cartographer: this map had been written in sweat and blood and death. . . .

"Here it is, Anders," the Swede was saying softly. "If you draw a line from Malaita in the Solomons to Makin in the Gilbert group, and if you bisect this line at three degrees south of the equator with a line drawn from Tongareva, you'll raise Vana Vana, Lost Lagoon. It's the loneliest stretch of sea in all this blasted ocean. Look—the atoll's shaped like a lobster, the claws reaching out to form the lagoon. The lagoon's roughly ten miles across and some seven wide. The five islets are fairly large. Here is the wreck —in about ten fathoms. Think of it! A king's ransom lies on the floor of Lost Lagoon!"

The fingers that held the edge of the map curled and uncurled, like a cat's claws. There was something feline in the Swede's eyes, too, with their subtle gleam and narrow pupils. Tor Jansen moved and his breath came sharply through his lips. Bergstrom straightened and laid a hand on Judd's shoulder. "Acquaint yourself with this ship, my boy," the man said quietly.

"You are navigator now. I have utter confidence in you. Lay your course for Malaita, in the Solomons. Red Malloy is waiting there for us with his diving gear and his men. Malloy's a fine diver. Crack on all the sail the brig will stand. We've no time to lose." He rolled up the map and put it away with care, almost it seemed with reverence. "You may go now. . . ."

When Judd regained the deck his brain was reeling with all that he had heard. As he paused by the weather shrouds the wind whipped at him, gratefully cool against his damp forehead. The boy took a deep breath and tried to shake himself clear of the recollection of that dim cabin and the two men crouched over the green-topped table. The seas slapped gently against the bow and the running light made a circle of glow in the blackness. At the helm the dark form of a native was barely visible in the light from the binnacle.

"Phew!" the boy muttered to himself. "I guess we're in for it! Wait till Ken hears all this! He'll forget to be seasick." He thought of his new-found friend lying wretchedly below and smiled grimly. "I bet he'll wish he was back in his blooming Museum before we're out of this."

For a moment he was swept with doubt and uncertainty. Then as suddenly as the swinging of a pen-
dulum his spirits surged upward. This—why, this was
adventure! He had supposed he was all set for California, yet here he was headed for the opposite
quarter of the Pacific. Headed toward mystery, and
perhaps even danger, whose outcome no man could
foresee.

Matu moved out of the darkness and laid a hand on
Judd's arm. His black eyes searched Judd's as he de-
manded: "What—what did they tell you about
Kassel?"

"Bergstrom said that Kassel died in sight of Tahiti,
of black-water fever. Is that true?"

"*Aita!* No!" came the swift denial. "Tor, the
Silent One, shot Kassel. Bergstrom helped to throw
him overboard."

"What!" Judd gasped.

"I saw it, I tell you! Have care—someone
comes. . . ."

In the shadows by the companionway a figure
paused, peering toward the two boys through the
darkness. A small figure with big ears, like a bat's. A
figure neither young nor old, with eyes alert and
glittering.

Tor Jansen stood watching them.

## CHAPTER IV   RED MALLOY

The *Island Queen* was a sturdy brig, well designed and stoutly built, of a rig not often seen today in the South Pacific. A ship perhaps fifty years old, yet it was evident that someone with a vast practical knowledge of the sea had had a hand in her reconditioning. The instruments for taking sights and soundings, the double sets of fine sails, the chart room and all its equipment, everything shipshape and in good order. There was no doubt that Bergstrom and his confederates had planned for a cruise of long duration.

In the two days immediately following their flight from Tahiti, Judd and Ken began to take stock of their strange situation and, with the adaptability of youth, to adjust themselves to it. They shared a cabin for'ard. It was so low that they could scarcely stand erect, and the foremast went right through the ceiling. The paint had turned black where a lamp swung in its gimbals. Two bunks were crowded into the corners; a washstand; hooks for gear screwed into the walls, that was all. But as the boys had no duffel they were aware of being cramped only when they tried to rise to full height. Already they had become firm friends.

Ken Henderson was in a seventh heaven of delight. The ship, the sea, the mystery surrounding this adventure, shook the dust of museums from his mind. He had recovered from his seasickness, and his zest for living knew no bounds.

"Do you know there isn't a blooming book but the log on this boat," he announced cheerfully the second morning out. From his pocket he withdrew his horn-rimmed spectacles. One of the lenses was cracked through, the other missing. "A memento of Sing Fat's," he explained with a happy grin. "I couldn't read a line if there *were* any books." Without his glasses his eyes had lost their look of vacant pre-occupation. "Say," he went on, "what's all this monkey business about, anyway? Where are we headed, and what for?"

"Buried treasure, my lad," Judd assured him solemnly.

"Oho! Fifteen men on a dead man's chest, eh? Doubloons, I gather, and pieces of eight?"

"No. A sunken steamer with a cargo of specie—gold, and a lost lagoon!"

"Phew! Is that all? No maidens held in durance vile?"

"Seriously, Ken, this is what I can put together: this brig belongs to Bergstrom and Tor Jansen. Who they may be, or where they come from, I've no more idea than you. There was a third man in with them named Kassel. But Matu told me that the other two did Kassel in off Tahiti. . . ."

"Killed him, you mean?" Ken's tone was incredulous.

"That's what Matu claims. He says that Tor Jansen shot him and Bergstrom helped to send him to Davy Jones' locker."

"But—people don't do things like that," Ken objected.

"Oh, don't they?"

"But why did they do it?"

"Perhaps to get his share of the plunder; perhaps to steal a march on him before he tried to pull the same trick on them. And maybe Matu was making the whole tale up, anyway; who knows? But they had to have a new skipper, which is why they put in at Papeete."

"So you were just the answer to a prayer?"

Judd heaved a shoe at him. "So it seems," he admitted. "Anyway we're steering a sou'-sou'-westerly course for Malaita, in the Solomons, where Red Malloy awaits us with his diving gear and some black boys. Then up anchor for Vana Vana."

"Vana Vana?" Ken queried.

"Our lost atoll, Professor."

Ken Henderson drew a hand across his forehead in the mock gesture of one who wipes off the sweat of astonishment. "Well, I'll be darned! Say, that Tor Jansen gives me the creeps. Those eyes always following you around. . . . And he can't make any more noise than a giraffe."

"It's no joke, Ken," his friend assured him. "These men may be out-and-out scoundrels for all we know. If this Red Malloy belongs to their outfit he won't be any better. We'll be in their power, three against two."

"But the Samoans would be on our side."

"True. But Malloy's bringing along some men of his own—black men probably. And Bergstrom sleeps on the key to the firearms locker."

"What's to prevent your sailing a course to the first civilized island instead of to this Malaita?"

"I've thought of that. But these men aren't fools: they can read a compass. If they're desperate enough to have done what Matu claims they did to Karl Kassel, they wouldn't hesitate to try the same trick with us."

"Then what's to prevent our deserting ship in the Solomons?"

"Do you know the Solomons?" Judd queried in the tone of one who talks to an obtuse child. "Malaita is just about as wild as they come. The two of us, unarmed, without equipment, wouldn't stand a ghost of a chance with the hill tribes."

"So you see no way out?"

"Not yet. . . . Anyhow, Ken, you'll have a grand chance to pursue your studies in Polynesian ethnology at first hand, what with a boatload of Samoans and Solomon Islanders and all."

"That's right! Two distinct and separate cultures." Ken smiled back at his friend happily. "You know, I've hardly thought about the Museum. They'll be

wondering where in heck I am and what kind of a
fellowship I think I'm working on; and probably be
sending cables to the Governor of Tahiti! But look—
I *have* done a bit of work already." He dove into his
pocket and produced a sheaf of notes written in pencil
on scraps of paper. Observations of marine life, of
sea birds, Samoan words chosen at random and spelled
phonetically; all manner of things that had caught his
professional interest. The five natives in the crew
were a source of unfailing wonder to Ken. Here at
last were his Polynesians at first hand and in the flesh.
Judd had accepted them without thought, as he
accepted the sea and the wind: he had known them
always. But the history behind these young Polynesians, the rich story of their people's migrations
from Asia, their origin and culture—these things he
had never even speculated upon. And these were the
very things that Kenneth Henderson had written
monographs about before ever he saw a Polynesian
in the flesh. Dimly Judd was beginning to understand
that he had as much to learn from Ken as Ken had to
learn from him.

Already they had made firm friends of the five
native lads on the boat: Matu, Terii, Taupo, Siva and
Falé. Toward Matu in particular Judd felt a warm
response. The youth was about his own age and spoke

Tahitian fluently. Judd's own knowledge of island dialects enabled him to pick up the Samoan tongue with ease, while even in these two days Ken Hender-

KEN HENDERSON

son set his scientific training to a study of the language.

"Well, there's nothing to do but go ahead and keep our eyes open," Judd concluded.

Next morning the two busied themselves with their special interests. Producing his inevitable scrap of paper and stub of pencil Ken would point to a rope or a bucket or an anchor and say: "What's this in

Samoan, Matu?" While Matu laughed good-naturedly at this foolishness of the white man, Ken jotted it down and stored it away in a memory trained to such things. He was picking up the difficult tongue with a rapidity that surprised Judd and astounded the natives.

Judd questioned each of the natives about the brig and her owners, but they could tell him little that served to clear up the mystery. The *Island Queen* had appeared in Samoa some three weeks before from Australia. She carried a crew of riffraff—water-front roustabouts who knew little of the sea. Kassel, who was in command, had discharged this crew and hired the Samoans. Then Kassel had died and was thrown overboard. That was all the native boys knew.

It was perfect sailing weather. The trade wind scarcely varied a handbreadth from day to day. "Flying-fish weather" the Samoans called it, and in all accuracy, for the flying fishes themselves fled before the brig, their flight a silver shimmer in the sun. Preyed upon by bonito, coryphene, and albacore, still their legions seemed inexhaustible. They were a never-ending delight to the eye. Dolphins were leaping about the ship like excited children released from school at that moment; surging, plunging, throwing themselves in parabolas toward the *Island Queen*, so close under the counter that it was easy to see the crescent-shaped valve of the blowhole whenever a head broke water. The sun flashed back from their varnished bodies; they rolled over lazily and dissolved in the mystery below.

The sky arched blue overhead, 180 degrees of it, and the *Island Queen* was the moving center of a limitless circle of blue. Judd had never beheld the grayer, greener seas of northerly latitudes. To him all water was blue water—a blue so intense in color that it seemed to have been born of a single vibration, forever and forever blue. And one day melted into another without so much change as comes from morning melting into afternoon.

Axel Bergstrom and Tor Jansen spent the long hot hours below in the after cabin. Their presence on deck seemed to dampen the natural good spirits of the Samoans. But when they were not in sight, and Judd and Ken were on deck with the five Polynesians, this mystery ship and her dark destination took on the glowing color of adventure. And then it seemed that things were surely not so dark as they promised. And the boys sang as they stood their trick at the wheel, and scrambled like agile monkeys up and down the shrouds, shouting for sheer joy in being alive and sailing down this fabled ocean. Since knowing Ken, Judd had come to realize how deeply he had missed the companionship of boys of his own race, how lonely had been a childhood spent among an alien people. Ken was—well, Ken was swell!

There was great excitement the morning that they raised an atoll: a low ring of coral rising but a few feet above sea level, surrounded by high-bursting surf. A smoke of gulls drifted above the trembling palms, their hoarse cries ghostly and unreal. It might have been one of the far-flung atolls of the Tuamotu group which scatter across ten degrees of latitude and a thousand miles of ocean. But Judd could find no trace of this one on the chart. It dropped out of sight as suddenly as it had appeared, over the curve of the horizon. Then the long monotony of the days remained unbroken. No sail, no far-off smoke. Only sea and sky and piled-up clouds whose trailing streamers told the direction of their passage. Dawn and sunset marked the flight of time: dawns as turbulent as the laughter of the gods; sunsets that painted the sky with the blood of titans.

And as the golden days slipped by, the mission of this mystery ship receded farther into the background of the two boys' consciousness. It was as if the searching sun, the clean air of the sea, sought out all dark corners and put mystery to rout. The crew was of easy-going temper, not to be driven too hard; capable of tremendous exertion when necessity called it forth, but they needed moments of relaxation, of fun. All the standing rigging had been tarred down, brightwork polished, gear set shipshape. Now out came the fishing tackle, and many hours were spent trying to persuade bonito or albacore to take the hook.

Judd, standing a trick at the wheel, looked for'ard along the deck where Matu and Ken were perched on the bowsprit trying to catch bonito. For days the great fish had been playing about the brig, frolicking, plunging, leaping in sportive capers. It is impossible to catch bonito from a sailing ship unless there is wind enough to send the ship ahead at a fast clip. Matu looked up at the sails, drum-tight in a racing breeze, and knew that a bonito was as good as landed. Judd, giving the wheel a spoke or two now and then, watched his two friends out on the bowsprit—Matu clinging by prehensile toes; Ken holding on by the grace of God. The native swung a stout line and hook that was baited with a twist of white cloth. He lowered the line, keeping the white cloth bobbing up and down just over the water. The rag attracted the bonito.

The fish leaped, was hooked. Matu hauled it up, struggling furiously. Ken swooped forward with a canvas sack and popped the thrashing bonito into it.

"*Aué!* How he struggled!" cried Matu. "Without the bag we should have lost him."

The fish's agile body and terrific struggles rendered it impossible to hold with the bare hands. As life ebbed in the floundering body its colors changed and shifted through a range of rainbow tints: steel-blue, cobalt, jade, and turquoise. Fish after fish fell before the skill of Matu, until ten or a dozen lay gasping out their life on the hot deck. They were a solid, compact fish, not unlike a large mackerel, with firm white meat.

"American, have you a silver coin?" asked Matu, shaking the salt water off his bronze hide like a seal.

"A silver coin?" queried Ken. "What for?"

"Because often the flesh of the *ahiahi* is infested with white maggots. It would be poison to eat. A silver coin boiled with the fish turns green if there is poison within."

"Of all the nonsense——" Ken, the scientist, began.

"Maybe not," Judd broke in. "These native notions are often grounded in hard fact."

Sea birds in legions were following the ship: albatross, gulls, petrels, boobies, gannets, frigate birds . . . Judd never tired of watching them. His father had known a great deal about such things—the fish and birds of the South Pacific—and he had passed something of his knowledge on to his son. The gannets, with their slim lines of head and body coming to a sharp point, were miraculous divers. There was one flying at a great altitude now, and the boys followed it with their eyes. They saw the bird suddenly fold back its wings against its sides and drop like a plummet into the sea. Within a second it emerged, a fish struggling in its beak. But conquest was not yet assured. For there was a frigate bird in the offing. The frigate swooped down upon the gannet—made it drop its catch. Before the fish fell back into the sea the frigate had turned with the speed of light and caught the fish in its beak.

"No wonder they're called frigates!" Ken exclaimed. "They're the pirates of the air."

"They can keep to the air for weeks at a time."

Judd offered. "And they're the only sea bird, as far as I know, that can't swim or dive. So they *have* to be freebooters to get food."

None of the birds seemed to show fear of the white-winged brig, taking her perhaps to be one of their own kind. And surely the stout little ship seemed at home in this blue element, responding like a creature alive to every mood and whim of the sea. Judd had never sailed in one of the great ocean-going steamers. But many times when they docked in Papeete he had gone aboard—up on the bridge or down into the engine room. Marvelous inventions of the human mind and hand they seemed to him—but ships? No! The noise of their propellers was enough to scare away every fish and bird for leagues of ocean. They were floating hotels, turbine-driven, where seamanship became a matter of bells and telegraphs. How could a man stand sixty feet above the water on a bridge and know aught of the sea? He had to be knee-deep in it, feel it swirling about him, filling his sea boots, putting the fear of God into his heart! At least, so thought Judd; and he remembered old Captain Joshua Slocum, said to have circumnavigated the globe in a forty-foot sailboat with no other chronometer than a Connecticut alarm clock. There was sailing for you!

Each dawn rose with a crash of color, and night fell softly as a footstep, while the *Island Queen* drew nearer and nearer to her destination: Malaita, in the Solomon group. Islands dark with mystery, these; home of cannibals and secret rites; of fevers and pestilential swamps, where black men move like shadows through the unimagined jungle. . . .

This part of the Pacific, known as Melanesia, is a network of more than two thousand islands. They stretch from a hundred degrees of longitude and from above Cancer to just below Capricorn—countless leagues of ocean. Some of the islands are no more than pin pricks on the Admiralty charts, but they are real enough to the anxious navigator. Melanesia is a vast sea-world which includes the Solomons, New Hebrides, Santa Cruz and Loyalty, Fiji, Bismarck, and New Caledonia groups. Micronesia is the second of the three great divisions of the Pacific: the belt where the Melanesian-Papuan strains merge with the Polynesian. Here are the Gilberts, Carolines, Marianas, Pelews, and Guam. The third group is Polynesia. And here are Tahiti—chief island of the Society Group—Cook, Ellice, Manihiki, Phoenix, Tokelau, Samoa, Tonga, Hawaii, the Marquesas, and the Tuamotus.

Of the three groups Melanesia is the most to be feared by the navigator; not alone for the race of head-hunters who people its dark shores, but for its incomplete charts and soundings, the uncertainties of harbors where earthquakes are forever playing havoc with the anchorage. It is a labyrinth of reefs where the signs of danger might easily be mistaken for the sea mirage, or an innocent and fortuitous shadow might simulate the threat of a genuine reef and warn off a ship to a safer course till she piled up on the actual and unsuspected rocks. It is a realm of treachery, deceit, and death.

All of Judd's previous sailing experience had been on long cruises with his father, where he had benefited by the older man's practical experience and knowledge, and the assurance of his presence in time of doubt or emergency. But now Judd was navigating through these badly charted waters with no knowledge greater than his own to rely upon. Sailing through the Tuamotus with their reef-spiked channels and erratic currents had been difficult enough; but in the Tuamotus there had been beacons and reliable charts, and first-hand information gleaned from schooner captains. The Solomons boasted few of these advantages. From northwest to southeast they extended across a thousand miles of sea. On all those miles of coasts there was not one lighthouse to give warning to the perplexed mariner. So the days passed

in anxious watchfulness. Judd was on deck from day-
light till dusk, and at night the brig sailed under
shortened canvas, with two lookouts wakefully alert.

The morning of the eighteenth day out of Tahiti,
however, was at first vastly reassuring to Judd Anders.
Far off, right where it should have been, the smoke of
Tanna's volcano rose into the sky, while off to starboard the island of Aniwa took shadowy shape. It
was the port of Su'u, on the west coast of Malaita,
where Red Malloy was waiting for the *Island Queen;*
and here, to Judd's sudden dismay, the Admiralty
charts used interrogation marks with disturbing fre-
quency.

The boy took a compass bearing of Tanna, another
of Aniwa. Then down in the hot chart room he laid
them off on the chart. Where the two bearings crossed
was bound to be the position of the *Island Queen.*
Then with parallel rulers he laid down a course from

the brig's position to Su'u. Having corrected this course for variation and deviation, he went up on deck. Tanna passed astern, silent and unreal, no more approachable apparently than a bright dream cherished in childhood, a dream which passed and was forever lost.

The coast of Malaita took dark, somber shape, its long valleys serrated with shadow as they flowed down to the sea. It was a coast rock-bound and forbidding, where a crashing surf burst in unbroken lines of white as far as the eye could see. All hands were on deck. Terii and Matu were at the wheel, Judd and Ken in the bows, Siva Falé, and Taupo at the masthead. Bergstrom, emerging at last from below decks, stood in the shelter of the after house, plucking nervously at his mustache; Tor Jansen lingered like a shadow at his side. The Swede's eyes were watching Judd Anders anxiously. How much did this boy know about navigation? Any fool could sail by dead reckoning across the open sea; but making port in the Solomons was something else. . . .

But Judd was unconscious of the man's concern. Through his glasses he was sweeping the rock-bound coast, searching for the opening in the reef that would lead into Su'u harbor. The brig ran in cautious parallel along the coast, driving ahead under a stiff breeze. Still

Judd could find no entrance in the reef. The tension of the Samoans communicated itself to him. Suppose —suppose he had made a mistake in his calculations? Of a sudden, uncertainty gripped him. He broke out in a cold sweat.

Then—there it was: the reef passage. Through the glasses the boy could see the seas breaking right across. Matu looked with anxious eyes from the surf to Judd.

The boy, straining desperately through the glasses, was hoping that the line of breakers from one side of the entrance would overlap the line from the other. Then—his heart pounded—he made out a narrow strip of water where the sea ran smooth.

"How's she heading?" he shouted.

"South-a-half east," came the answer.

"Let her come up south-by-west. Got it?"

"Got it."

". . . and a-half west," Judd amended.

"A-half west," came Terii's echo.

"Hold it—steady!"

Judd sped back along the deck. "I'll take the wheel, Terii. Help Matu and Siva with the fore-stays'l, and stand by to let go." He put the wheel down and steadied for the entrance. *Now!*

Through the passage the brig tore, the reef yawning hungrily at them as they fled. Afterward, Judd grinned to think that on the Admiralty chart of Malaita a mile of rock-bound coast stretched across this very passage where the brig had sailed!

The little harbor of Su'u opened up before them. It was as still as a pond. Dark trees closed in around it in a solid wall. There was no wind. The beach was a thread of light between the green lagoon and the somber forest. Surely no man ever had landed here. There was nothing living in sight but the frigate birds, black shapes high overhead with angular pinions outstretched and motionless, soaring in the slow leisure of timeless spirits. The anchor chain rattled through the hawse hole with a hollow reverberation that echoed back from the gloomy hills. Scarcely had the anchor settled on the sandy bottom before two long black canoes were putting out from hidden places in the mangroves. With conflicting emotions Judd and his friend watched them approach. Bergstrom, white with suppressed excitement, swung one arm in a wide arc of salute. A lean figure in the forward canoe made an answering gesture. Tor Jansen stood motionless by the mainmast, blinking in the strong sunlight. It occurred to Judd that the realm of sun and light was not Tor's element: he belonged somehow to a submarine world of octopal gloom, a world shadowed with mystery.

"That must be Malloy!" cried Bergstrom, eagerness edging his voice. "He's got plenty of gear all right."

The second canoe was paddled by four naked savages, the sun glinting on their black skins and barbaric ornaments. A pile of boxes and canvas sacks filled the center of the canoe. The white man reclining at ease in the leading canoe made no further gesture after saluting Bergstrom. In the prow of his canoe there stood the statue of a Melanesian in a breechclout, and the statute became alive as the canoe disappeared under the brig's counter where a rope ladder was hanging. Next, a pair of hairy freckled hands appeared at the rail. A man, a white man, was pulling himself aboard. Red Malloy. . . .

## CHAPTER V   THE PAINTED ALBATROSS

So you're Red Malloy," were Bergstrom's first noncommittal words.

"That's me, Axel. And I'm glad to shake yer 'and, not 'alf."

By his accent the newcomer was Australian: the half-cockney intonation peculiar to most Australians save those who school in England. Red Malloy greeted

Bergstrom and Tor Jansen with a wary cordiality. It seemed to Judd that there was suspicion, uncertainty, in the man's glance. The boys studied him with interest. They saw that Malloy was above medium height, with the sinewy build of deceptive strength; perhaps fifty years of age, yet there was youth in the lithe quickness of his movements. The man's bright greenish eyes seemed to take in everything at once; they were close set to the bridge of his longish nose, which gave him a crafty look. There was shrewdness in those eyes, and obvious intelligence. He was dressed in shabby ducks and a grimy *topi;* a two days' growth of beard glowed dull red on his lean jaws, while his skin—the sort which never tans—was the hot hue of a boiled crayfish. An irregular scar stretched from his right cheek bone to the corner of his mouth.

As Malloy's eyes fell upon Judd and Ken Henderson they opened in surprise, then narrowed swiftly. "Didn't know as we was shippin' passengers," he growled truculently. "Where's Kassel?"

"Kassel's dead," came Bergstrom's answer.

"Dead?" Malloy caught him up quickly. " 'Ow's that?"

"Black-water fever," the Swede replied briefly. "This is our new skipper, Judd Anders, from Tahiti."

"Hmmm! So Kassel's dead. That leaves us pardners-three, eh, Axel?" It seemed to Judd that there was a note almost of relief in the man's tone.

Tor Jansen was still standing by the mainmast, motionless; he had made no effort to greet the new arrival or to impress his presence on the scene. Malloy turned to survey him. "And you're Tor Jansen," he said softly, his glance traveling over the meager figure. "I've 'eard about you, plenty." It was evident that what Malloy had heard was uncomplimentary, nor did he relish what he saw. Hostility seemed to leap like a spark from his eyes, while far back in the pale eyes of the other a light glittered and was instantly extinguished. But Judd had caught its meaning, and again a thrill of apprehension shivered along his nerves. He knew hatred when he saw it. These three men, partners in a strange and dubious adventure, would not pull together smoothly; there was no doubt about that.

Malloy swung about and gave Judd an appraising measure. "And you're *Mister* Anders, our skipper. My eye, but you're just out o' the cradle! Does yer mother know the company you're keepin'?"

The boy felt himself grow warm with anger and he clenched his fists. Ken laid a restraining hand on his friend's arm. Bergstrom moved into the breach smoothly: "The lad is only a kid, Malloy, but he's had a lot of sailing experience. He'll do."

"Righto! He can keep on navigatin' for all o' me," Malloy returned airily. "I'm a steamer man, I am, and I don't 'old much with these sailin' crates. If you get in a jam though, my lad, just call on me. I know these waters like the back o' my 'and. Say, Axel, 'ow about a spot o' scotch? Think it'll do me any 'arm? I'm as dry as a clam at low tide."

The two men moved off toward the companionway with Tor Jansen following as silently as a shadow at their heels. With a feeling of relief the boys watched them disappear. The air seemed clearer with their departure.

Malloy's six Solomon Islanders stood about uncertainly, surveying the ship and her crew from little eyes deep-set under receding brows. They were an incredibly dirty lot, and far from engaging in appearance. Their noses and ears had been pierced with grotesque ornaments, their teeth filed to points. One had inserted the top of a tin can in the lobe of his ear; another wore a china doorknob on a string around his neck, while a third had thrust the tail of a pig through the cartilage of his nose. They spoke a gibberish that was unlike any dialect Judd had ever heard—guttural sounds that might have been the origin of all human speech.

Judd ordered them to haul aboard the two canoes,

remove the outriggers and stow them on the fo'c'sle head with strong lashings. The blacks set about the task passively. The muscles of their backs and shoulders knotted with the strain of hauling the two big canoes to the deck of the *Island Queen*.

Ken Henderson was bursting with ethnologic delight at this opportunity to study at first hand still another Pacific race. "Look at those canoes, Judd! Did you ever see anything like them?"

"They're beauties, all right," Judd acknowledged. "You'd never believe they could have made them. From the looks of them you'd say they couldn't figure anything out."

The canoes were dugouts, beautifully proportioned, with high-curving stems that had been decorated with shells and strange devices. There was a fineness of proportion and line that attested the beauty of all supremely functional things.

As the blacks filed forward dragging the canoes after them, Judd noted that each man had a sheath knife fastened to the cord of his gee string, the blade sharpened to razor-edge and gleaming wickedly. The Samoans looked with disgust upon these eaters-of-men, as they called them.

"Pigs, whose ancestors were pigs," muttered Taupo as the blacks passed for'ard.

"Stow that, Taupo," Judd warned. "We'll have enough trouble without your inviting it."

The native boy was silenced for the time being, but the rest of the Samoans were muttering, too, and Judd knew that it would not be easy to keep peace between these discordant opposites. A ship is a small world. On the *Island Queen* there were now sixteen people who would be shut up together within the space of a few feet, undergoing heat, thirst, poor food, the nervous wear of storm and calm. These things caught men on the raw, reduced tempers to high explosive, magnified small grudges into burning hatreds. With Red Malloy's arrival, the *Island Queen* seemed to have become a floating powder magazine waiting for a spark to touch off the explosion.

"Say, Judd, what do you make of Malloy?" queried Ken.

"I don't quite know," his friend replied thoughtfully. "I can't figure him out. One moment he seemed like a ruffian, if ever I saw one; the next I felt something about him——"

"I know," the other assented. "There *is* something about him. You have a feeling that he might have gone straight if he hadn't taken a wrong turn somewhere; while Bergstrom and his buddy were born crooked."

"That's it. Say, did you see the look Tor Jansen gave Malloy?"

"Did I, though! There'll be trouble there all right."

"You know, Ken, I have an idea that Bergstrom's not a Swede at all."

"What do you mean?"

"I believe he's a German. Kassel certainly was, for there's a book on navigation in the chart room that's written in German and Kassel's name is on the flyleaf. As for Jansen——"

"But if Bergstrom's a German," Ken interrupted, "why should he be passing himself off as a Swede?"

"I don't know," Judd admitted. "But I've an idea about Kassel—just a shot in the dark: this wreck we're looking for was sunk by a German submarine, and my hunch is that Kassel may have been on that sub! Most of those Germans were interned in New Zealand after the Allies took over the German Pacific islands, and they've been kicking around the South Seas ever since."

"Say, you've got something there," Ken agreed excitedly. "Why, Kassel might even have been the sub's commander."

"I thought of that one, too. Who knows?"

"Well, we're in for it, Cap'n. Down the bounding main with a crew of pirates," crowed Ken. "Ethnology was never like this!"

"If we don't walk the plank before we get through

we'll be lucky," Judd muttered. "No telling where this'll end!"

"But you didn't want to go to college anyway," Ken came back at him with a grin.

Judd smiled wryly. 'I know I didn't, Ken. I couldn't see what my dad was driving at when he wanted me to leave Tahiti. But since I've known you I—I think I begin to understand."

"How's that?"

"Oh"--Judd hesitated, unable to find words to express his thought—"perhaps it's just that there's a whole lot more to life than sailing a schooner and diving for pearls. You have to learn things. Accomplish things."

Ken nodded. "Brains are tools, Judd: they've got to be developed and sharpened and used. A college degree doesn't mean any more to me than it does to Matu; but a heck of a lot goes into earning that degree, and don't you forget it. Sweat and brain and heart and discipline. Your dad was right."

"Say, you're not going to preach, are you?"

"You bet I'm not, you nut. But I'm right and you know it."

Judd, standing by the rail at his friend's side, looked out across the darkening water and made no answer. He was beginning to understand much that he had scarcely troubled to think about before. Ken *was* right. And when this strange adventure came to an end, he would have to try to fulfill the high hopes his father had held for him. He would work, and learn, and accomplish.

RED MALLOY

By sunset Malaita had dropped below the horizon. Its mysterious hills folded in upon themselves, harboring their dark secret. Night crouched just over the peaks of the mountains and the *Island Queen* pointed her eager nose directly nor'-nor'-east.

Vana Vana, Lost Lagoon. . . . Did it really exist? Anything, Judd admitted, was possible in this

loneliest of oceans. He knew—as what sailor does not
—that space has been dwarfed for the landlubber by
geography books. Their neat scales of miles render
the Pacific Ocean no more formidable than a mill
pond. Men who spend their lives in office or factory
see the Pacific only as page 87 in their school atlas,
unmindful that it covers more than a third part of the
globe, and contains within its vast periphery over
half the waters of the sphere. But to the sailor, *El Mar
Pacifico* means thousands of leagues of storm-tossed
sea, where disaster lurks just over the horizon, and far
down below, the locker of Davy Jones is filled with
the bones of luckless ships.

Standing there by the rail, watching Malaita dis-
solve into mystery and darkness, Judd thrilled to the
courage of those early Pacific voyagers who had set
sail upon an unknown sea. He remembered that it
was Vasco Núñez de Balboa, courageous governor of
the Spanish colony of Darien, who first had learned
from his Indian friends of a vast ocean lying to the
west. Crossing the Isthmus of Panama in 1513, Balboa
was the first European to behold the ocean to which
he gave the name, Great South Sea. It remained for
Magellan seven years later to call the sea *El Mar
Pacifico*, after sailing for many weeks over its calm
waters from the Straits of Magellan to one of the

Tuamotu group. For years thereafter Spain and Portugal were the only rivals in the Pacific. But today Spain owns not so much as a palm tree in the great ocean, while Portugal controls but a sliver of Timor, in the Malay Archipelago.

In the vast Pacific thousands of islands lie scattered, ranging from the world's smallest continent, Australia, and second largest island, New Guinea, to tiny pinnacles of palm-crowned coral. Most of the islands lie in lonely reaches of ocean that are never visited from year's end to year's end. The traffic of nations keeps to well-defined sea lanes. Modern Admiralty charts are miracles of cartography, but even on these there are many islands which have an interrogation mark placed after their names, bespeaking the uncertainty of their position, their very existence. Already Judd had experienced something of this at Malaita. He knew that there are islands which have been marked in all definiteness and have been sighted but once, while others that have figured boldly on Admiralty charts have been omitted from current maps, since painstaking research has proved them to be nonexistent.

Judd recalled Falcon Island, one of the more recent discoveries in the Pacific, which had fascinated his father: a veritable hide-and-seek island. First sighted by H.M.S. *Falcon* in 1865, it had disappeared from sight of men by 1898. Within thirteen years the sea had caused an island two miles in diameter to disappear completely! But as recently as 1927 the H.M.S. *Laburnum* reported that a submarine eruption had raised the island high above the sea. Now it was marked on all maps in latitude 20° 19′ S. and longitude 175° 25′ W.

Yes, anything was possible in this lonely ocean, and as the two boys stood there watching the darkness lift up from the face of the sea, to Judd at least the existence of Vana Vana seemed suddenly real and actual. As if his companion had read his thought Ken asked: "Do you suppose there is actually an island called Vana Vana, Judd?"

"Yes, I guess I do believe it, Ken. But whether I can pick it up from Bergstrom's chart is another matter. The *Antipodes* sank twenty-five years ago and bearings taken under those conditions may not be accurate. If this were a 'high' island the problem would be simplified. But an atoll that rises only a few feet above sea level can easily be passed by, even on a clear day. We may go sailing around in circles and never find it. And the farther we get toward the equator, the more variable the weather. The doldrums are no fun—not when you're looking for a lost island, and fresh food and water aren't too plentiful."

"Vana Vana lies in the doldrum belt?" Ken asked.

"Just over the edge of it, according to the map." The boy turned to Matu, who was lounging by the rail, a pandanus cigarette hanging from his lips. "Have you ever heard your people speak of a great atoll lying to the south and east of Samoa?" he queried.

Matu scratched his head and wrinkled his brow in thought. "I have heard the Old Ones sing in their chants of an atoll to the south and east," he finally replied. "An atoll that lies in a devil's region of reefs and currents. *Aué!* American—it is not there that we are going?"

Judd nodded. "It may be only an Old One's tale," he answered. "Only time will tell."

North and south of the equator there is a region known to charts and skippers as the "area of calms and variables"; a region of exasperating weather where winds and currents act according to their own whim without recognition of any known laws. As the *Island Queen* moved into this region the wind dropped imperceptibly while the thermometer climbed toward the sky.

Bergstrom and Tor Jansen spent the hot days below in the main cabin, playing cribbage. Bergstrom was a poor loser and his confederate was unfailingly lucky. As he played, the Swede's voice floated up through the transom interminably through the hot hours: "Fifteen-two. Fifteen-four. Fifteen-six . . ." It was a blessing, Judd thought, that Tor Jansen couldn't talk; at least they were spared the sound of an added voice. Tor Jansen: the boy's mind dwelt for a moment upon that strange shadow of a man. Who knew what forces had twisted him into the creature that he was, or what distorted fancies gnawed at his wretched soul? Sometimes at night the gnomish form emerged from below decks and moved about the ship like an uneasy wraith, a shadow reft of its substance. Locked within his prison of silence Tor Jansen set the men's nerves on edge. There was something almost piteous about him, like a sparrow with broken wings. Judd had lived in the South Seas long enough to observe what those lonely islands could do to even the most rugged of white men. The heat, the blasting sun, the isolation from ties of tradition and heritage that bind civilized men into gregarious communities, often took odd vengeance on those who turned their backs upon the country of their birth. The bones of such men strewed the beaches of the South Pacific like derelict ships. Bergstrom, so unlike his strange companion in every outer respect, treated Tor Jansen with a sort of protective consideration, while Malloy seemed to stand apart and alone, unable to bridge the chasm of antagonism which existed between them.

During the long hot days the Samoans lay listless about the decks, seeking such shade as offered. There was no need now to touch sheet or stay, and the inertia of the elements descended upon the natives' spirits, making them moody and fretful. Malloy ordered his blacks to rig up an awning from a length of sailcloth. Under its hot shade the man took his ease in a deck chair, a dead pipe hanging from his lips, while sweat poured from his sinewy body in streams that fell on the hot planking in little pools and evaporated. He was stripped to shorts, and his feet were bare except for a pair of old blue slippers which hung limply from his toes.

"Blast me!" he cursed one morning, as the sun climbed the tall sky and the decks became a searing ache to the eyeballs. "Only six o'clock and look at that bleedin' thermometer! 'Ell itself don't get 'ot afore noon."

Ranga, his body servant, crouched beside his white-fella-boss on the blistering deck, seemingly impervious to heat. He was devoted to his master. The black boy was of indeterminate age, scarred by battle; his only clothing a meager loincloth and a necklace of empty cartridge shells. He conversed with Malloy in *bêche de mer*, that strange language evolved by white traders and used throughout Melanesia. It was a language as peculiar to that region of the Pacific as the Chinook lingo is to Alaska, and it had been born in the same way.

The labor recruiters, the pearl traders, and the missionaries had manufactured a tongue suited to the limited intelligence of the savage.

Ken was fascinated by it, made up as it was of words which served many different meanings.

"It's like a game," he told Judd. "For example, nothing stands alone. Everything's related. 'Knife belong you; foot belong me.' And *walk about*, I don't know what they'd do without that expression! If a sail has to be furled the order is 'That fella sail walk about too much.'"

Judd grinned. "And today when Ranga was seasick

I heard him say 'Belly belong me walk about too much.' "

*Bêche de mer* had grown little by little into a recognized language, and the two companions were getting no end of fun out of using it.

Red Malloy rose from his deck chair and walked aft to the poop where Judd was standing a trick at the wheel. Ranga padded on silent black feet after his master. Matu saw them coming, flung his cigarette overboard, and moved across to the lee side of the poop; the Samoan had small liking for this white man and his eaters-of-men.

"Hello, young fellow my lad," Malloy greeted Judd. " 'Ow about a bit of a chin-wag to pass the time? It don't seem exactly sociable around 'ere, and that's a fact." Settling himself comfortably against the binnacle, where a strip of shadow from the mains'l broke the sun's glare, he scratched a match and brought his dead pipe to life.

Judd gave the wheel a lazy spoke and forced a smile. "It's this weather—it's hard on everyone."

Malloy wagged his head sagely. "I been sailin' these seas nigh thirty years, but I ain't never got used to doldrum weather. Fair drives a man crazy and that's a fact. It ain't so bad when you've got decent company—but it's a couple o' fine pardners I picked," he finished on a note of complaint. "Treatin' me like I was a poor relation."

"You must have seen quite a few islands in thirty years," Judd remarked.

" 'Ave I though! Ain't an island in the archipelago I ain't put in at, one time or another. I've taken my ship into 'arbors where they wasn't supposed to be no 'arbor! Red Malloy's a sailor from way back."

Judd disregarded this modest claim and asked the question that was uppermost in his thoughts: "Does Vana Vana really exist, Malloy?"

"Reely exist?" His companion turned to survey him with wide eyes of astonishment. "What do you think we're takin' this trip for—a bank 'oliday? Exist, you ask? Didn't I make a chart of 'er? Cripes—I was cast away on 'er, and let me tell you the only good thing about it was that my missus couldn't follow me there. You ever been married?"

Judd shook his head.

"That's right. Steer a clear course o' them reefs. Thirty years I've 'ad of it and it's tough sailin'. My wife was born a lidy, if you know what I mean; 'er father bein' Controller of Sewage Disposal in Sidney, and I never 'eard the end of it. She felt she'd lowered 'erself takin' up with a bleedin' sailor, and she'd go on and on and on, until I'd be fair minded to give 'er a paste in the jaw, lidy or not. I run out on 'er four times, and Vana Vana was the only place she didn't find me." Malloy chuckled with relish at the recollection of that triumph. "She *couldn't* find me there, because nobody knew where the blasted island was. And wouldn't it be my luck to be the only man out of eighteen to come back alive? I figured maybe I'd find the missus married to someone else. But she was waitin' for me. She'd never given up 'ope, she said."

"Where was it she did find you?" Judd asked, intrigued in spite of himself.

"Once in Singapore, once in Manila and once in 'Onolulu. Would you believe it? Just as I'd be feelin' all 'appy and relaxed-like, up she'd pop like a jack-in-the-box and she'd say, 'Fancy meetin' you 'ere, you sweep!' Always the perfect lidy. I tell you"—he jerked a lean thumb toward the after cabin—"those two blokes below are welcome to the gold! I'll take me freedom. Once I set foot on Vana Vana I'll never leave it again except in irons."

"So you were the only man out of eighteen to return alive to New Zealand?"

"That's right, m'lad."

"Bergstrom told me that that man's mind was a blank, and he couldn't tell anything about the sunken ship."

"Did he now?" the other returned warily. "Fancy

Axel callin' my mind a blank! Small wonder though, if it was. You ever been in an open boat for ninety-five days, under a broilin' sun, with the food gettin' scarcer and scarcer and finally runnin' out, and water down to the last jugful?"

"No, I haven't."

"I 'ope the Lord in 'is infinite mercy will never bring you to it, my lad. Yer lips crack and yer tongue swells and the skin dries up on yer bones. And if ye never prayed before in yer life you begin to pray then. Not for deliverance, no; you pray for rain. And you sit there with your blinkin' mouth open like a pelican, 'opin' for a drop from 'eaven to fall into it. Ye see men turned into animals, snarlin' and snappin' at each other like a pack of dogs. Ye see 'em droppin' off, one by one; jumpin' overside, or bashin' out their brains on a thwart, or tearin' at each other tooth and nail. You begin to 'ear voices in the air around you, over your shoulder, down the wind . . . and faces deep in the water lookin' up at ye, and 'ands beckonin'. . . . And me with nothin' to look forward to if I *did* live, except the missus. Aye, small wonder if a man goes through it and comes out, even to 'ave his mind a blank."

"How did you manage to take such accurate sights and soundings at Vana Vana without instruments?"

Malloy flashed him an artful look and parried the question. "Ain't you the dinkum little sleuth?" His face closed and grew hard. "Say . . . how come you and the professor joined up with a pack of rogues like us?"

"It was no choice of ours," Judd assured him.

"Blast me, are you the touchy one!" Malloy's eyes, so bright a green, blazed with a sort of playful, sardonic irony.

Judd found himself filled with curiosity concerning this man. There was a sort of foxy geniality about Red Malloy that made it impossible wholly to dislike him. He was not unlike a thousand others of the variety which Judd had seen washed up like flotsam on the beaches of the South Seas. Yet there was something subtly and indefinably different about him: a hardness of fiber, a toughness of spirit, which set him apart from that army of derelicts. As the man stood there on wide-braced legs he looked fit and hard, and long years in the tropics appeared not to have softened his compact frame. The scar across his cheek was livid and ugly and, it seemed to Judd, too recent to be of long standing.

"How did you come by the scar?" the boy asked curiously.

Malloy's lips twisted in a sly grin. "What would

you say if I told you a German bayonet got me, in a skirmish on the Somme, back in '16?"

"I'd say it must have been exciting."

"Just what I thought you'd say. As a matter o' fact it wasn't a bayonet: an army mule kicked me in the jaw. An Allied mule, at that. But you couldn't tell the folks at home a thing like that. Heroes ain't kicked by their own mules in war time."

"That scar of yours doesn't look twenty years old to me," Judd said shortly. The man was lying and he knew it.

Malloy's eyes converged in the swift look which transformed his face. "Ho! Sherlock on the trail, eh? Listen, young feller, don't go pokin' yer snout into things as don't concern you, savvy?" He thrust forward his chin at a bellicose angle, glared at Judd, then turned and ambled back to his deck chair; he sank into it with a weary curse and lighted his dead pipe.

Judd looked after him with puzzled eyes and shook his head. He felt that he knew no more about Red Malloy than he had in the beginning. The man was a deep one all right, playing a long game. The boy gave it up and turned his attention to the business at hand, giving the wheel a spoke or two, and whistling vainly for a puff of breeze, while through the transom Bergstrom's monotonous voice rose on the dead air: "Fifteen-two. Fifteen-four. Fifteen-six. . . ."

Sharks had begun to appear, as they do about a ship becalmed: dark shapes dim in the fathoms. Standing there at the wheel, Judd could see the great fish circling slowly around the brig or lying in the shadow of her side, watchful and alert. Each shark had its inevitable escort of pilot fish, striped like harlequins, swimming just ahead of the shark's jaws. There was one ponderous old hammerhead that the boy was beginning to recognize: its skin looked like gray burlap and it kept pace with the ship with scarcely a perceptible motion of tail or fin. Something in the sinister suggestion of its patience began at last to get on Judd's nerves. The boy eyed the grappling hook, half tempted to have a go at the hammerhead, but he refrained. For he knew that the Samoans would have small sympathy for such an act, and would look upon it as a portent of bad luck. To them sharks had a significance tinged with the supernatural. They would kill one in self-defense if attacked, but they would never seek the encounter.

At the rail Judd saw that Taupo was muttering half aloud the words of an old chant to *Ma'o*, the Shark God: a chant so ancient that the exact meaning of its words is lost.

*"Ma'o é! E matài tu! E matài ta. Ma'o é!"*

Did Judd imagine it, or did the hammerhead give

the merest flicker of his tail as he lingered in the cool shadow of the hull?

Sea birds were appearing once more, too, bespeaking the fact that there were islands somewhere over the rim of the world, and not too far away. Judd handed the wheel over to Matu and lounged lazily at the rail, watching the fine flight of an albatross high in the upper air. What a magnificent creature it was, the very king of sea birds. Its power of flight is miraculous; it can hang in the air for hours at a time, seemingly without movement, but its prodigious wings outdistance the fastest clipper, while no gale is too strong to find the bird floating serenely in the sky, scornful of a wind of eighty-mile velocity.

As the boy stood there, looking up into the blue sky, he felt a deep contentment flood his being, an inner certainty that whatever befell him was part of an ordered design. The things that had weighed upon him—selling out the plantation to Wong Fu, going up to the mainland—that all seemed as far off as eternity. He was here on the deck of this fine ship with a wide sky blue-arching overhead. This was his life. This was what he had been born for. One of these days he would have to leave it behind for a while, but in the meantime he meant to enjoy it to the full. What more could any boy ask than this—a fine ship to sail, a friend

like Ken, companions like Matu and Terii. . . .
What did Bergstrom and his dubious companions
matter? Judd drew himself up straight and slim and
faced the sun. His shirt and ducks were ragged
and patched and thin with many washings; his hair
had been bleached to the color of a ripe banana, and
in the rich brown of his skin there was more than a
hint of Polynesian blood-gold, against which his eyes
blazed like an Anglo-Saxon sky.

Ken, too, had developed mightily as the days
passed; the hollows in his cheeks had filled out, and
his pale skin was darkly tanned. Judd watched his
friend indulgently. Ken was sprawled in the shadow
of the fo'c'sle with his inevitable stub of pencil and
scrap of paper. Notes. Ken was always taking notes.
It was as if a world which had existed only in his imagination had suddenly taken material form, and he
found it still hard to credit, and infinitely more exciting than imagination ever had painted it.

This ocean, this blue radiance, was a realm where
men were unaware of the urgency of the outer world,
where there was only the creaking of unseen gear and
the monody of the waters; masses of weed drifting
past with its ancient smell, as if you could sniff the
antiquity of the sea. This was a voyage beyond the
counting of mere days. Time did not exist. The blue

swells, diminishing to infinity, the bright heaven, the silence except for the hiss of the cutwater—they were the lure and dream of every boy who ever stood on a ship's foredeck and looked beyond the horizon. The horizon beckoned and they followed, but its hard line was inviolable. It could not be passed. Each hour it receded farther, like good fortune when pursued.

Judd smiled at the thought of the monographs that Ken would write when he got back to his Museum; and his heart warmed with affection for his American friend. He had known few such in his remote island life, and in the short time they had been together on the *Island Queen* they had come to know one another better than would have been possible in months of life ashore. No—Judd was more convinced than ever that if there were more fellows like Ken on the mainland, going up to the University wouldn't be so bad!

"Look, American!" Matu at the wheel spoke from a corner of his mouth. "What devilment is the Silent One planning?"

Judd turned to see that Tor Jansen had emerged from the companionway; the man stood there, slight and stooped, blinking in the sunlight. Ken looked up from his notes, watching curiously. Even Malloy twisted half about in his chair while Ranga hushed his apelike chatter. They saw that Jansen carried an iron hook shaped roughly like a diamond, fastened to a length of stout line. He moved over to the rail and scanned the upper sky with a strange intensity. Involuntarily every eye followed his gaze. There was a tensity of purpose in the man's action which caught and held them all. Far overhead, white-gleaming against the blue, they saw that the albatross still wheeled and planed, and Tor Jansen was watching it.

"*Aué!*" cried the Samoan in consternation. "He plans to catch the albatross!"

Terii echoed his concern. "The Great White Bird harbors the souls of drowned sailors," he muttered. "To catch it will bring bad luck to us all."

Now Tor Jansen was fastening a strip of salt pork around the edges of the diamond-shaped hook. There was a curious intentness about him, an inflexible resolve; it seemed almost as if the king of sea birds, float-

ing so serenely in the blue above, were a force which
he must bring to earth and cripple, that he might himself find life endurable. He sidled over to the rail with
the gliding octopal movement which characterized all
his actions. He cast the line overboard. It trailed out
behind the ship, the white pork bobbing invitingly on
the dark swell.

High overhead the albatross lowered its angle,
planed swiftly down, closer and closer, until Judd
could see its gentle questing eye turned upon the
treacherous bait. Then swift as light the bird dove for
the pork—seized it. At once its beak was caught on the
diamond-shaped wedge. Quivering now in his excitement Tor Jansen began to haul in, hand over hand,
keeping the line taut so the albatross could not break
free. The bird splayed out its feet to retard its passage through the water. Judd was hoping fervently
that the bird would manage to free itself and take to
the air. Red Malloy watched intently, an inscrutable
look on his hard face. The Samoans stood about, filled
with concern; Ken's lips were drawn with disgust.

Jansen hauled the bird up out of the water; he
seized it by the neck and lifted it over the taffrail. The
albatross, so magnificent in the air, flapped about on
the deck in a helpless fashion. Its wings thrashed
violently as it tried to rise, but the hard deck planking

rendered flight impossible. Its captor, moving with the same swift tensity, tethered the bird to a stanchion, then disappeared down the main hatch.

"What do you say we cut it free?" Ken suggested.

But before Judd could reply Tor Jansen reappeared. They saw that he carried a can of red paint and a paintbrush. Crouching on his knees before the terrified albatross, he proceeded to paint a large red cross on the snowy breast of the bird. The cross was as startling as a cry in the night. Jansen, with his brush, circled around, shifting and feinting as he dodged the bird's sharp beak, then darted in and seized the struggling body. There was something terrible and grotesque about the warped little man struggling with that magnificent bird. He dragged it, panting, to the rail—managed to drop it over the side into the water.

The albatross hit the sea with a splash, bouncing for a helpless moment in the swells. On its snowy breast the red cross stood out, vivid as a smear of blood. Instantly Judd was aware of a whir and fury in the sky above. Half-a-dozen frigates, diving like arrows, hurled themselves down upon the painted albatross. Within ten seconds they had hacked and torn the bird to pieces. A few white feathers drifted on the air. A circle of blood widened in the foam. . . .

Tor Jansen gripped the rail with both hands, shaking with spasms of silent laughter. What happened next came as a complete surprise. Red Malloy rose from his deck chair. The scar on his jaw stood out as livid as a wound. Reaching the laughing man in two swift strides, he seized him by the back of the neck.

"You bleedin' image of a white man!" he rasped through his teeth. "Get aht o' this! Lord 'elp you if I ever catch you at it again!"

Malloy shook his victim as a terrier might shake a rat. Tor Jansen twisted about, powerless in the grip that held him. His mouth fell open in a ludicrous gape of amazement. His head, bobbing back and forth with its batlike ears, might have been filled with sawdust. It seemed that his neck must snap.

At that second Axel Bergstrom emerged from the companionway. "*Malloy!*" The Swede's voice ripped the silence. "What's the meaning of this?"

Malloy flung Jansen to the deck. Without answering he pointed to the widening circle of blood on the foam.

"A strange role for you to play, Malloy." Bergstrom's tone was deadly cold; his eyes were like ice on fire.

Malloy started to reply, thought better of it. He stamped noisily aft, muttering under his breath.

Tor Jansen lay where he had been thrown, his face half hidden in the crook of a protective elbow. Now he lifted his head and looked after Malloy's retreating figure. His lips moved soundlessly; sweat ran down his face, like tears, into his mouth. He tried to shape a curse. His throat thickened. Then there issued from his throat a sound of painful ragged breathing—the first sound Judd had ever heard pass his lips. There was something gruesome about it, an animal sound that had no place in the speech of men. But there was no mistaking its meaning or the message in the man's eyes: it was as though a resentment that had been gnawing on his mind and heart for years of helplessness were at last breaking through the surface in a torrent of sheer hatred.

Bergstrom helped him to his feet with hands that were curiously gentle. Jansen clutched at the arms that supported him, and in his humiliation at what had happened it seemed to the two boys that he attained a certain aloof dignity. He clutched at Bergstrom's arms as though he were trying pitifully through a gesture to attain an understanding he could never reach through words. The Swede guided him below decks while the boys and the Samoans stood rooted to the deck, staring stupidly after them.

"Well," Ken breathed, when the men had disappeared, "what do you make of that?"

"It looks as if we'd been right: Malloy has a decent instinct in him after all."

Ken shook his head. "Jansen will never forgive him for this. If Malloy doesn't get shoved off into the sea I'll miss my guess. Malloy's a funny combination of good and bad."

"He's a deep one," Judd admitted. "Yesterday I found him in the chart room studying the chart of Vana Vana."

"I should think he'd know that by heart," Ken broke in. "He's supposed to have made the chart, isn't he?"

"That's what I told him, and all he said was, 'It's 'ard to 'old fathoms and soundings in your 'ead for twenty-three years; I was just brushin' up a bit.' It sounded fishy to me, and after he'd gone I found a scrap of paper on the floor. I picked it up and it read: 'Anchorage 100 yards off E. Coast in 6 fathoms.' "

But Ken was paying no attention to Judd's words. He had started forward, then stopped and gripped his friend's arm. "Look, Judd! What's that?"

Judd followed the line of Ken's forefinger. With an exclamation he picked up his glasses.

"*Aué!*" cried Terii. "*Faariri!* A waterspout!"

It seemed no more than a vague point of cloud, cone-shaped, dropping to meet the horizon. But

through the glasses Judd could see that it was growing rapidly, a formidable column of whirling water. It
rose some two hundred feet in the air. Toward the
*Island Queen* it swept, moving at incredible speed.
Half a mile away they could hear its roar.

Judd's voice sang out: "Call all hands!"

## CHAPTER VI  MEN AGAINST THE STORM

T HE AIR WAS a vacuum. The brig slithered on a
sea of glass. Nearer, nearer came the waterspout,
its outlines darkly defined against the sky. A noise like
the roar of a blast furnace moved with it, mounting
as it approached in wild crescendo. So overwhelming,
so formidable, that those on the *Island Queen* held

their breaths, as if by that involuntary action they might avert catastrophe. The whirling column possessed a fascination that gripped them in momentary thrall, rendered them speechless and without thought.

Of a sudden the brig heeled over. Her starboard rail lay in the water. For one terrible moment the waterspout hung over her, all but toppling. The little ship would be annihilated. There was no escape. . . . Then, not fifty feet to starboard, the vortex passed. Slowly the brig righted, still lying quiet in that awful calm.

"*Aiá!*" whispered Matu. "Never have I seen a *faariri* so large!"

"I have heard my grandfather tell how the great *Moana* was struck by one," Falé offered. "All aboard were drowned."

The heat was overwhelming. No hint of freshness livened the air. Cat's-paws whipped up out of nowhere like blasts from an open oven. Sweat poured down the backs of the Samoans who hung about the decks, waiting for the action which was sure to come. The *Island Queen* lay motionless, her spars thrusting up idly into the dead air. Immense clouds walled the sea, inclosing the brig in a glittering clammy heat. As one hour merged into another, the metal brightwork became too hot to touch; the pitch between the deck's

planking bubbled and stuck to the men's bare feet.
The sun was like a malignant eye set in a socket of
infinite space. Overhead, the canvas hung lifeless from
the yards; the only sound was the rasp of the parrels
as the brig rocked gently on the smooth swells. Bergstrom emerged from the companionway, his face
strained and nervous. Taupo whistled hopelessly for
a wind, but the brig lost steerageway and the Samoan
lolled at the wheel.

"God, it's hot," Bergstrom muttered.

"Profanity's no 'elp," said Malloy. "I've tried it.
'Ow about a drink?"

"You drink too much."

"Bli'me! A little wine for the stomach's sake is a
Scriptural injunction. I 'ave no doubt that applies to
good Scots. Not that I 'old with 'ard drinkin', you understand. It's a low 'abit. But it fills the 'eart with good
cheer, and softens the blows o' misfortune." He spoke
with the smug assurance of a man whose rich uncle
has died and left him a fortune.

Bergstrom stood silent. The lack of friendliness between the two, Malloy had tried in vain to bridge with
forced joviality. But his attack upon Tor Jansen had
widened an irreparable breach between them.

The ship was motionless, except as she drifted back
and forth in the grip of some unknown ocean current.

Not a quarter of a mile away two whales heaved their varnished hulks half out of the sea; jets of watery vapor were spouted high into the air with a long-drawn hissing. So vast was their bulk, yet so leisurely their movement, that scarcely a ripple disturbed the water as they submerged.

Judd knew that the waterspout was only a prelude to storm, since the barometer had behaved erratically for two days past. The brig herself seemed to feel the menace in the air and squared off for battle. The boy felt her response and quickened to it. Ships to him were things alive: ribs, planking, skeleton, shroud, and stay—the whole fabric seemed but the nerves and sinews flexing in response to a higher command. The *Island Queen* had long since won his heart with her clean sailing. Should disaster overtake her—by storm or by reef—it would be to him a personal loss. Grand little ship. . . .

Bergstrom was wiping the sweat from his forehead with nervous fingers. "The bottom seems to have fallen out of the glass; 29-50 she stands now; going down and pumping at the same time. I don't like it."

Tor Jansen had remained below. Malloy lounged indifferently in his deck chair; he appeared completely unconcerned, even though Ranga crouched whimpering at his side with animal awareness of approaching storm. Occasional puffs of breeze began to make themselves felt, fickle and exasperating. At the first whisper of wind Judd gave the order for the heavy yards to be dragged around to take its full advantage. But no sooner had the sweating men braced up the yards than the mocking breeze shifted about and came from the opposite point of the compass. Then it was, "Weather forebrace!" and the weary men threw down the freshly coiled gear and hauled round the yards to the new tack. In short, it was the "area of calms and variables" running true to expectation.

A sudden flare of lightning was followed by an instantaneous crack of thunder. Without warning the heavens burst asunder. Rain struck in stinging sheets. It rattled on the decks like shot upon parchment; torrents of water, pouring down with such intensity that the men could see scarcely a dozen yards ahead. The ocean hissed under its impact. The men plugged up the scuppers, letting the deck fill with fresh, sweet rain water. Water casks and barrels were opened, allowed to fill anew. Every available pot and pannikin was set out to catch this blessing from the skies. The Samoans discovered forgotten bits of soap, scoured first themselves, then their belongings. Soon *pareus* and ducks hung limply from every shroud and stay.

As suddenly as the storm had broken, it ceased. The sun shone forth through a rift in the clouds, while the *Island Queen* steamed from every pore. The threat of some natural and overwhelming force, held in reserve, hovered like a cloud over the brig and over the men aboard her.

"Do you think we're in for real trouble, Judd?" Ken asked anxiously; for he was always seasick in rough weather.

"It'll have to get worse before it's better—like a cold in the head. You might as well turn in now and be done with it."

"Guess I'll stick it out on deck," the other replied quietly. "You may be needing me."

"There's enough of us to take care of things. You'd better go below. Malloy's an experienced seaman and I can call on him if I need him."

But Ken remained on deck, although his face was already taking on a greenish tinge and there was misery in his eyes. "Wonder if I'll *ever* get used to it?" he muttered.

The sky deepened in weight and grew more lowering. Thunder clouds, rising high, were urged forward by some wind that scorned the lower levels. Judd was sweeping the eastern horizon with his glasses. Now he lowered them. He stood beside Taupo at the wheel. "Here she comes," he said.

Like the advance scouts of an army, wind flaws harried the water. Behind them, moving relentlessly forward, the sea was a sharply defined strip of wind-whipped darkness. Waves were rising, shouldering at one another, their crests spitting and hissing. Then with a howl and a roar the squall struck; wind rushed in like a screaming siren. The *Island Queen* heeled over to a sharp angle. Slate-colored seas swept over the brig, pinning her down. She wallowed sluggishly, unable to clear her decks of one sea before another rushed aboard. The heavy pounding shook her to her keel bolts. She trembled in all her ribs, but she took the smash of each sea with grim determination, watching for the next. She met battle like an experienced old fighter, stiff in the joints but stout of heart, and onward she lumbered.

Judd, tight-lipped and anxious, strained to hold the wheel with Taupo. Matu stood beside them on wide-braced legs, one ear cocked above the whistle of the wind to catch and transmit orders. Terii was amidships; Siva and Falé on the fo'c'sle head, tuned to the pitch of storm.

Bergstrom appeared at Judd's side, struggling to keep his foothold on the slanting deck. "Give her more canvas," he cried, "and put about! Maybe we can outrun the curve of the storm."

More canvas? The man was crazy. Judd paid no heed. The wind shifted a point, bringing in a mighty squall. The fores'l split with a roar that could be heard even above the howl of the elements. The wildly whipping canvas was ripped to shreds—swept away on the wind.

"Did you hear me?" the Swede yelled furiously. "Do as I say! Put about!"

"I'm in command!" Judd shouted back at him. "Matu, clew up the maintops'l—rout out the Solomon Islanders!"

Matu passed the order on to Terii. The native fought his way for'ard, his hoarse voice yelling: "All hands! Shorten sail!"

Bergstrom took half a step toward Judd, both fists clenched.

"Don't be a blasted fool!" rapped Red Malloy. "We need that lad!"

Slowly the men made their way up the swaying rigging. Out over the futtock shrouds, hanging on by a miracle and the grace of God. Now they were out on the yard, fighting to conquer. The heavy sail fell upon them, burying them with its weight. They fought for life on the pitching yard. One second's pause in the wind, the merest fraction of *respite—now!* Straining over the yard on their bellies, feet hooked into the lifts, they beat at the canvas with clenched fists, trying to batter a dent in it, a grip for bleeding fingers. Both hands for this work! At any second they might be hurled into the sea. But they held no thought for that. There was only this banging, slatting monster-canvas that would destroy them if it could. Naught below but a whirlpool of seething water; no sound in their ears but sea and wind. Torn fingers and tortured muscles fought that canvas. Seconds were like hours.

At last the sail was on the yard; made fast. Double gaskets looped. Everything secure above. They slid wearily down the shrouds.

The Solomon Islanders, routed out of the fo'c'sle, whimpered like scared monkeys but leaped to do as they were ordered. Bergstrom clung to the weather ratlines; the swinging seas, the wild wind struck terror to his soul. He was afraid to go below, afraid to stay on deck. Fear sagged his face, stared from his hollow eyes.

Lightning streaked the sky. It ran to the ends of the yards, struck at the hissing sea. In the awful second of its being it revealed a waste of tumbling water: mountains moving in wild flight, black in the hollows, livid on the slopes. The cresting tops were torn off and flung back at the sky.

The storm increased its fury. Judd and Taupo, wrestling with the wheel, could not get the helm up.

"Malloy!" the boy shouted hoarsely. "Lend a hand with this wheel!"

Malloy paused uncertainly, laid hold of the wheel. He was as awkward as a landlubber. The wheel bucked violently. Malloy was thrown to the deck. Judd looked at him with incredulous eyes. This man—mate of the *Antipodes!*

"Lay hold!" the boy shouted again. "What's the matter with you?"

"You blasted fool!" Malloy flashed back at him. "I ain't no sailor!"

A smoking sea thundered over the length of the brig, drowning Judd's reply. He and Taupo clung to the wheel with the desperation of life and death, fighting it for control. Before the ship could clear herself of one inrush she was raked by another. She lay trembling, stricken, trying to shake off the load on her back. Fighting with all her power, still she yielded. Down, down she was forced. Water leaped upward through her lee scuppers.

A wall of water rose ahead. Many they had seen, but this wave towered higher than them all. Its crest heaved over with a vast sigh. The brig shoved her nose into it. The Solomon Islanders screamed their terror. The ship's masts jerked forward with a snap that set the guys vibrating like plucked strings. Wire and timber groaned. Then the stern swung high into the air. A murderous sea caught her thus off guard and slewed her round into the trough. Down, down she sank, shuddering at the threatened blow. Seas broke over her poop and rushed forward. Judd and Taupo, half submerged, gasping for air, clung to the wheel with the desperation of life and death. Ken and Malloy sprang into the shrouds. The Samoans took to the upper rigging. Bergstrom, torn from his hold, was swept across the deck. His voice shrilled out above the welter. He fetched up against the lifeline. There he clung, burying his head.

The *Island Queen* rose again. She was weary now and shivering in every timber. Then back she fell, heeled over as if by a giant's hand. Her yardarms seemed almost to scoop the waves. In the trough for one interminable moment she lay, on beam-ends. Rigging cracked and snapped. T'gallant masts bent like whip handles. Somewhere in the brig's structure would be an imperfection, one weak link which would prove her undoing. How much could this balanced fabric of wood and metal stand?

With a crash the lifeboat was wrenched from its davits—swept away like a chip on a mill race. Only a

miracle saved the wheelpost and the two men clinging to the helm. Judd knew that the brig could not
last much longer under such punishment. Somehow,
somehow, she must be hove to if they were to live out
the day. But to have brought her broadside at this
moment would have spelled the end for them all.

Minutes lengthened. . . . White-lipped and grim
the boy watched his chance to bring the shoulder of
the brig to the sea. There came a momentary lull—one
second's respite out of chaos. *Now!* Down the helm!
Terii leaped to lend a hand. Three boys, waist-deep in
swirling water, fought the bucking wheel. Into it went
every ounce of strength, every atom of hope for survival. . . . The brig needed but a second's grace
under the grip of her helm; wind-pressure would drive
her forward.

"Head sheets—let go!" Judd's shout was hoarse.
"Ease off lee braces—haul in!"

Siva flung the order for'ard. The head sheets were
let go on the run. For a second there was only a mad-
ness of banging chainsheets, thundering canvas, groan-
ing spars. But the brig responded. Lurching, pitching,
masts swinging across the sky, out of the trough she
lumbered. She staggered drunkenly, but her standing
rigging held. The *Island Queen* lay hove-to, safe for
the time being. Bergstrom, disentangling himself from

the lifeline, felt cautiously along the deck toward the companionway. His face was gray and nerveless as he crept below.

The worst was over. Toward dawn the gale moderated, blew itself out . . . weary men fell asleep almost where they stood, a deep thankfulness in their hearts.

As for Red Malloy—now that the storm was over and Judd had time to think, the boy remembered that astounding moment when the erstwhile mate of the *Antipodes* had acted like the veriest greenhorn at the wheel. There had been defiance and desperation in the man's eyes as he looked back at Judd Anders. "I ain't no sailor!" he had said. Well, what was he then? *Who* was he?

The *Island Queen* fled on the heels of a rousing breeze, laying knots behind her. She was wearing canvas wherever an earring could be bent. Water boiled white along her lee rail. Judd had taken his noon observations, worked up his sights. Now, back on deck, he scanned the horizon with anxious eyes. Vana Vana should be some twenty miles to the northeast. Picking up this island out of thousands of leagues of ocean seemed like searching for the proverbial needle. Doubt lay heavy on the boy's spirit.

Off to the northeast a faint haze glimmered along the horizon, the merest shimmer of light. Sometimes the lagoon of an atoll throws up just such a haze. Judd's pulse hammered. Could it be? Perhaps he only imagined it. . . .

Matu gripped his arm. "*Aué!* American. *Te mori!* The lagoon light!"

"Judd! Judd!" shouted Ken. "There she is!"

"Yes, but——" the boy faltered.

Then high and clear from the masthead rang Terii's triumphant shout: "Land ho-o-o! Land ho-o-o!"

Judd sprang for the main ratlines, shading his eyes against the sun. Far off, faint and vague in the white light of noon, lay something that was neither sky nor sea. The swells, lifting higher, now showed now concealed it. Far off, but surely there—an atoll known only to the gulls and gannets and the ghosts of Davy Jones's locker.

Vana Vana—Lost Lagoon. . . .

## CHAPTER VII  LOST LAGOON

T HE SHIP WAS in pandemonium. Bergstrom rushed
on deck, his face alight with triumph. Tor Jansen moved swiftly at his heels. The two men stood by
the ratlines, scanning the shore line with binoculars,
and Judd noticed the trembling of their hands. Malloy
sauntered up the companionway, his green eyes spar-
kling with foxy malice.

"Bli'me!" the Australian exclaimed. "Does that land

look good to me! Though it wouldn't surprise me none to see the missus sittin' under a palm tree waitin' for me. She's that nosey-parker!"

The Samoans were shouting excitedly and running from one side of the ship to the other. *Fenua!* Land! Fresh food to eat. Look—there were breadfruit trees, and palms by the thousands. . . .

The sun shone through a luminous mist, casting a sheen like a dust of gold over the sea. High up, a pageant of clouds moved across the sky to shadow the circlet of land below them. Running smoothly before the wind, the brig's canvas swelled to the racing breeze. With each passing moment the atoll took on form and color. Its foliage glistened in the sun like green lacquer; on the barrier reef the surf smashed and pounded with long-drawn roar, sending up a mist of rainbow tints into the tremulous air.

Judd put Matu at the wheel and climbed higher up the ratlines, searching the shore line for the three pandanus trees that, according to the map, marked the reef opening. Down the coast of the atoll the brig fled like a startled deer. Gulls screamed at the masthead; the sky was alive with them—hundreds, thousands, their raucous cries piercing through the thunder of the surf. With thumping heart Judd picked up the three pandanus trees. They leaned like tired sentinels over the passage.

"Ready about!" came the boy's call.

"Ready about it is!" followed by a rapid paddle of bare feet on the deck.

Then Judd again: "Hard alee!"

"Hard alee it is!"

The yards swung round with ease. There came a rattle of ropes running through the blocks. A rousing chantey rang forth as the Samoans hauled on the braces:

> "*E moua roaroa*
> *Faanunu mai raro e!*"

For one moment the *Island Queen* seemed to pause as she came up into the wind; then the wheel went over to the grinding of the rudder chains, the sail filled slowly, shook out the wrinkles, and swelled drum-tight. Then like a homing pigeon the little brig headed straight in through the narrow reef passage. So close were the coral walls on either hand that almost it seemed as if those on board could reach out and touch them. Spray leaped high. Treacherous currents pulled and eddied. The whole island rushed to meet them.

"The anchorage is a 'undred yards off the east coast in six fathoms," offered Red Malloy.

Bergstrom said, "You've got a good memory, Malloy." And his tone was grudging.

"Fer details," Malloy answered loftily.

Judd threw him a quick look. He remembered the scrap of paper on the floor of the chart room; he remembered the man's failure at the steering wheel. Malloy was a deep one, all right.

"Heave the lead, Matu!" the boy ordered. "Stand by to let go, Siva. What do you get, Matu?"

"Six faddom."

"Let her go, Siva!"

The anchor chain grated through the hawse hole. The *Island Queen* came to, spilled the wind from her sails, took a deep breath, and relaxed in every timber. She was in safe harbor at last.

In the heat-shimmer of the coral shingle the island threw back a jewel-glitter of unbelievable brilliance; light struck from above and below, bleaching all shadow with its brightness. For a moment those on board the brig were struck silent with wonder. After weeks of the sea's long monotony they seemed to behold a geological dream: a vision of the land as first brought forth, fresh with beauty, in the world's beginning. The lagoon stretched away and away like a vast mirror, reflecting a blue sky swept with mare's-tails. Its oval was enclosed by five densely wooded islets. Those to the south and east were some ten miles away, while the *Island Queen* lay in the protective lee of the largest islet to the northeast. In the clear green deeps alongside, sharks were patiently patrolling for anything that might happen.

Malloy, never to be downed for long, clapped Axel Bergstrom on the back with high ebullience. "We're bloomin' well 'ere!" he crowed.

Bergstrom drew away from him slightly. The Swede and his silent shadow seemed to have come to an understanding which no longer included their boisterous partner. "Vana Vana hasn't changed much in twenty-four years, has it, Malloy?" was Bergstrom's cool reply.

"Don't look exactly over-populated, and that's a fact. But I won't feel easy until I've 'ad a chance to look around a bit. Wouldn't surprise me none to 'ear 'er sweet voice sayin', 'Fancy meetin' you 'ere, you scut!'"

Bergstrom scanned the surrounding shore line through his glasses. "Order the boat out, Judd. I want to look around."

Judd gave the order. He left Terii, Siva, and Falé in charge of Ken on the brig. Malloy, Bergstrom, and

Tor Jansen climbed down into the lowered boat, where Matu and Taupo manned the oars, with Judd at the steering-sweep. The Swede held the chart spread out on his knees as he directed the way to the sunken wreck. Judd, standing in the stern sheets, followed the tortuous line of the channel as it twisted its devious way through the coral patches.

So clear was the sky, so calm the surface of the lagoon, that the lifeboat seemed to slip through a blue vacuity, leaving but a transient furrow to mark its passage. A group of stingarees fled at their approach, flapping their wings like aquatic bats; the steel-gray dorsal of a shark followed them in leisurely parallel. Fish leaped high into the air to fall back with a resounding splash, while startled birds rose from their nesting places, croaking hoarsely. Life teemed beneath the pellucid surface of the lagoon and in the air above it. The dense growth of scrub and palms that covered the ring of islets looked as if it had never before been disturbed by man.

Bergstrom was scanning the bottom of the lagoon, intently, through the water glass. Suddenly his breath caught. "There she is!" he cried excitedly. "And right where she's supposed to be!"

They all peered over the gunwale, hearts beating high. Sixty-odd feet below, in the twilight of the lagoon floor, the wreck of the *Antipodes* lay like a broken shadow.

"You, Matu," Bergstrom ordered, "see how things look below. We'll get out the diving gear later."

The native adjusted his goggles—a crude affair made of orange wood with pieces of glass gummed into the openings, forming water-tight compartments. Then he slipped a sheath knife over his head and climbed into the water. Clinging for a moment to the side of the boat, he breathed deeply several times; then down he went, feet first. At about four fathoms he turned over and swam toward the bottom with powerful strokes. Twenty-five, thirty, thirty-five, forty feet down—the men in the boat could follow him as he descended. But soon in the mysterious blue of the greater depths his figure blurred, then vanished altogether. It seemed an interminable time until they saw him ascending again, rapidly, his breath coming up ahead of him in clouds of escaping bubbles.

Matu's black head broke the surface with a splash. He clung for a moment to the gunwale, chest rising and falling sharply, his eyes bloodshot and his face strained.

"*Aué!*" he gasped. "She lies deep!"

"Is she on an even keel?" Bergstrom demanded in a tight voice. It was with difficulty that he held himself in control.

"*Ai!* Yes!" came the youth's answer. "But there are holes in her sides. The sea has done its work."

"Crickey! It fair takes me back," muttered Malloy. "Seems like yesterday. . . . Us prayin' for the Lord's 'elp to reach this lagoon before the ship sank under us; and us not used to prayin', neither."

Bergstrom's eyes were glowing with avarice. "It looks as if our trip would be a success, Malloy. To-morrow morning we start work with the diving gear. We're wasting no time."

"The sooner the better," Malloy agreed. "I 'ope the sharks in these parts don't go for gold. It'd be a blasted shame to 'ave all this work for nothin'."

"The gold's there all right," Bergstrom said softly. "It's as good as in our hands."

Tor Jansen sat on the bow thwart, his face twisting. Wealth lay almost within his grasp—gold. With gold he could buy men's respect, force himself upon an unwilling world. . . .

"I'd like to take the outrigger and a couple of men this afternoon," Judd put in, "and prospect around a bit." He saw Bergstrom's eyes narrow in swift suspicion, and he added: "There may be fresh water on some of the islets; perhaps turtle or wild pig. We'll need fresh food."

The Swede's face cleared. "Look around by all

means. We've water enough for several weeks if we're careful of it, but we'll need fresh food. Malloy and I will have the men get the gear in shape while you're gone."

When the lifeboat returned to the brig the three men disappeared below, obviously to celebrate their good fortune. Ken and the Samoans crowded around Judd, plying him with eager questions. Judd's heart was beating with excitement. He had noted that the sandy bottom of the lagoon was lined with small shell, while in the shallows he had seen masses of fernlike water whips, which were always considered a sure "sign" in the pearl islands of the Tuamotus.

"I believe there are pearls in this lagoon, Ken," he declared eagerly. "We're going to do some diving on our own account! But first we'd better explore a bit so the men won't be suspicious of us."

There was a canoe, shorn of its outrigger, lashed to the roof of the fo'c'sle. Now willing hands cut the lashings, set up mast and rigging. The canoe was a Samoan dugout, some fourteen feet long and scarcely more than a foot wide. Without its outrigger it would have capsized within a second. Terii rigged a spritsail that would have seemed out of all proportion to one who did not know these sailing canoes. So large was the head that no common sprit could have carried the strain of it in an ordinary breeze. With Matu's help, Terii lashed a spar to the canoe, letting it project aft over the stern. To this spar he then made fast a sprit-guy: thus the foot of the sail was held by the main-sheet and the peak by the guy to the sprit. They lowered the canoe into the water. Judd and Ken dropped into it, followed by the two Samoans. The other boys stood at the rail shouting encouragement after them.

The canoe flashed across the water like a streak of light. Judd climbed out on the outrigger to lend his weight for ballast. Terii, too, climbed out part way, while Matu steered with both hands and held the mainsheet with his toes. Ken sat on the floor amid-ships, bailing furiously with a coconut shell. "Hey! Slow down a bit!" he yelled. "I'm sitting in water!" But as well have tried to slow down an iceboat.

The breeze freshened, and across the lagoon the outrigger fled, on a balance as precarious as that of a tightrope walker. Judd had sailed these canoes all his life, but he had never seen one handled with the skill and nerve which Matu now displayed. From Judd's slender perch on the outrigger he could look down into the water, deepening and shoaling under the canoe in patches of vivid or vague color, and so clear that all scale of distance was confused. It might be

forty, fifty, sixty feet deep. Gardens of branching
coral opened up beneath them, where schools of fish
gleamed and darted like submarine butterflies, and all
the rainbows of the world there found authentic end.

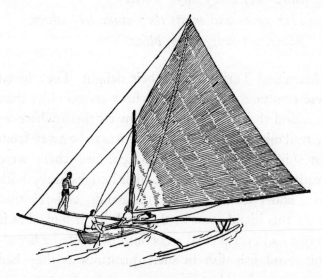

Now they were tearing across some darker channel
where flying fish skimmed in silver clouds. Soon a
bank of sand jutted into the anchorage where the
*Island Queen* lay, and as they rounded the point the
brig was lost to view. They were alone in their island
world.

Judd drew a breath of deep content. Streaking
across this wide lagoon with the salt wind in his
nostrils and the blaze of distant beaches in his eyes, he

felt like a boy again, playing at pirate with his dusky crew. Ken was singing at the top of his lungs:

*"Oh, a Yankee ship comes down the river,*
*Blow, my bully boys, blow!*
*Her yards and masts they shine like silver;*
*Blow, my bully boys, blow!"*

Matu and Terii grinned their delight. They loved these two young Americans who were no older than they, and they would have followed them wherever the trail might lead. How good it was to be away from that ship and those eaters-of-men! See—there were breadfruit trees on the shore, their boughs heavy with fruit; and coconuts by the thousands, and *fei,* too! Truly this island must be deserted, for it looked as if no one had ever picked a coconut or roasted a breadfruit. And fish—fish in such quantities as they had never seen. *Aué!* but this was a paradise for sure.

The fruit trees of Vana Vana attested two facts: the previous visitation of sailing ships, and a soil of great antiquity.

"Are atolls always as full of vegetation as this one?" Ken was asking. "I thought——"

Judd shook his head. "I've only seen one other like it: Nanorik, in the Marshalls. The Tuamotus are just the opposite. In the old days, when there were lots of people, they were always having famines."

"Which probably explains why the Tuamotuans were the only Polynesians to be cannibals," Ken supplied.

"*And* the Marquesans!" Judd reminded him slyly. "You're slipping, Professor!"

Ken laughed. "*We* won't have to turn cannibal. Look at the fish—millions of 'em!"

"Yes, but you have to be careful about the fish, Ken. In these atolls a fish that's good eating in one island will be poison in another. Or often a fish that's poisonous if caught in the lagoon will be safe to eat if you catch it in the open sea."

"Great Scott! How's that?"

"The natives say it's the moon that regulates the season of good fishes. Personally, I think the changes are due to phases of the coral—for coral is poison itself."

"But can't the native tell which fish is good and which isn't?"

Judd shook his head. "Not unless he's on his own island. If you transplant him to a strange one he's as helpless as a greenhorn. It seems to be a matter of time and place."

There is no distinction in nature more broadly marked than that between the "high" islands of the Pacific and the "low." They are as different as the

Rocky Mountains and the Sahara Desert. The "low" islands, or atolls, are as flat as soup plates: mere circlets of *motus* threaded on a reef to enclose a lagoon. At their highest point they rise scarcely higher than a tall man. They are at the mercy of wind and tide and sea: the work of a tireless marine animal—the coral polyp. The shores of Vana Vana were not rock; they were organic: half alive, half putrescent.

"American, it will seem good to have fresh coconuts once more," Matu was saying.

"And pigs, perhaps," added Terii hopefully.

"If there are pigs they must have been brought here by men," Matu reminded him. "Pigs were never in these islands before the white man came."

"True enough," Judd agreed. "Perhaps some old skipper marooned a mutineer and left him a pig or two for company. If so, we'll feast high."

"Roast pig, cooked underground in the *umu*," sighed Matu, and his mouth watered at the golden prospect. He could fairly see that pig wrapped in fragrant *ti* leaves, steaming in its bed of hot stones.

"And those eaters-of-men have been too long without meat," Terii suggested with a sly smile. "We had better find pig!"

"Why do you suppose Malloy brought the blacks?" Ken asked. "They're not divers, are they?"

"No," Judd answered. "They haven't the courage or the spirit for diving. I believe the only reason he brought them was to have a standing army behind him."

"Maybe he's counting on them to pop us off when the time comes," Ken suggested.

"They'll be needing us, or me at least, to get them back to Australia, or Singapore, or wherever they're headed. They can't do anything without a navigator."

"But Malloy was first mate on the *Antipodes*, Judd. He ought to be able to navigate."

"Maybe . . . but just between you and me, I don't believe he knows his lead and latitude from a lamp-post. He's playing some deep game of his own."

"What kind of game?"

"I've no more idea than you. But he certainly doesn't hit it off with his pals, and I've a hunch they're suspicious of him for some reason."

"He'd double-cross his grandmother if it would be any advantage to him," Ken said, "and Bergstrom and his buddy know it."

"There'll be blood spilled between them yet," Judd added dubiously.

"Those eaters-of-men are no good divers," Terii was saying with vast scorn. "Only *my* people know how to dive to the lower depths of the lagoon."

"*Parau mau*, that's true," echoed Matu. "I have been one hundred feet without diving helmet. And once I went one hundred and fifty in the white man's diving suit."

"For myself, I will dive without the suit," said Terii. "Always I feel as if I would smother in those helmets. Give me my knife for the sharks, but do not shut me up in those terrible suits."

As the canoe drew closer to the distant *motu*, the boys scanned the beach for some sign of life. But the vegetation grew in choking profusion to the line of the sand. The coral clinkers threw back a glare of blinding ferocity. The scene was indescribably wild and lonely, touched with a sense of isolation beyond anything in Judd's experience. The boy found himself wondering what it must have seemed like to the castaways of the *Antipodes*, marooned here in utter solitude.

In most Pacific atolls the distance from the lagoon beach to the ocean beach is but a few hundred yards. The ocean side is unbelievably solitary. On quiet days, when the surf is lazy and the tide is on the ebb, the silence there is overwhelming. Men marooned on such an island, with naught but sea birds to keep them company, must indeed be tough to survive.

Matu spilled the wind from the sail and ran the

canoe up on the beach; its prow cut into the sand with a soft crunching sound. Judd and Ken leaped into the shallows and ran toward the shore. For the first time they were setting foot on Vana Vana! As far back as Judd could remember he had heard tales of hidden lagoons, rich with a loot of pearls. Old schooner captains had yarned about them with his father. Mata Afa talked about them over the evening fires. The boy had listened as a child listens to fairy tales, knowing with a part of his mind that they were not real, yet enjoying the notion of them more deeply than ever he would have enjoyed the actuality. Now here he was, standing upon the shores of just such an island. A thrill swept through him. As for Ken—he was like a bloodhound on the trail, poking into the vegetation, turning over coral boulders as if he expected to find there hidden some message which would tell him the origin of the Polynesian race. He was all ethnologist now, oblivious to the world of actuality about him. Every shell, every stick and stone spoke a language that he understood.

"If Vana Vana lay in the path of the ancient Polynesian migrations," he was muttering, "we'll find *maraes* and burial grounds and artifacts. . . ." There was no bounding his enthusiasm. Petroglyphs and pictographs, artifacts and trilithons: these were the things he'd given his life to. And here on this far island who knew what might not be discovered? What hidden stone or abandoned implement might be the missing link in the mysterious chain of Polynesia? Ken was like a race horse restive at the tape. . . . Judd watched him out of the corner of his eye with vast amusement. How different Ken was in his own element! How certain and sure and serious. The boyish, carefree companion had become all scientist, heedless of the world around him.

Matu and Terii trotted on ahead. The heat was intense: it shimmered over the glaring sand and lent to the distant palms the appearance of an unattainable mirage. Turtle tracks caught the boys' eyes. Somewhere a wild boar crashed through the undergrowth, causing Matu to crow with anticipation. Birds, nesting, rose in startled flight, to swoop down at the intruders. The boys shook sticks at some that, darting too low, threatened their eyes with questing beaks. Hermit crabs scurried away at their approach, snapping into their shells to make fast the door with a tinkling sound among the coral clinkers.

Matu was as frisky as a colt turned loose to pasture. There was no curbing his high spirits.

"I will show you a trick, Americans," he chuckled, "a trick we play on the hermit crab in Samoa. Watch!"

He picked up half-a-dozen empty shells and laid them in a circle. Then he caught a live crab, taking hold of its claws quickly before it could retreat into its shell. He maintained a steady, gentle pull on the claws. At length the muscles of the crab's tail began to tire; its grip relaxed. With a little jerk Matu extracted it from the shell. The naked crab's first attempts to walk were ludicrous and set them all laughing. The shell had weighed some four times more than its occupant, and the crab appeared as bewildered as might a man from Mars adjusting himself to a new law of gravity. The crab dashed toward one of the shells in the circle, made a suspicious inspection with its feelers, found something apparently not to its liking. On it moved, to inspect the next shell. This one seemed satisfactory. The crab turned about and in it went, tail first, shifting around inside for a second or two like a man trying to settle a new coat on his shoulders. Then, well content, the crab scurried off up the beach, while the boys followed it with their laughter.

A flock of parakeets darted overhead with piercing, whistling cries, while a small gray bird flitted to the top of a *tamanu*, entirely unafraid of the strangers, and sang a song of joyous, lilting measure.

The boys halted to listen.

"What is it?" Ken asked.

"A *komako*. They're rare in the inhabited islands, although the old people say there used to be lots of them."

"Do they always fly alone?"

"Except in nesting season. Listen! Isn't that a lovely song?"

The notes rose in liquid flight, incredibly sweet and true.

"It's like the song of the cardinal that we have at home," Ken said. "You'll be hearing that, Judd, one of these days."

The boy laughed, impatiently. "Just at this moment I don't care if I never do," he answered. "Isn't this swell, Ken? Look at that lagoon! What more have you got to offer in America? Gangsters and movies and labor riots!"

Ken laughed back at him good-naturedly. "It's not all like that, you nut!"

A sudden whir of wings in the undergrowth brought the boys up with a start. Next they heard the high-pitched crowing of the jungle cock, for all the world like the familiar barnyard greeting of civilized fowl. Through the trees the boys saw a wild rooster with the sun glinting on his fine red plumage. With a beat of wings the bird sped away, *tuk-tuking* in alarmed anger. But a mother hen with a brood of chicks stood her ground, ruffling her feathers while her offspring scurried into the jungle.

"Chickens!" Judd exclaimed. "Well, I'll be darned! Who'd have thought it, *here!*"

"I'll bet their ancestors were brought across the Pacific from the East Indies a thousand years ago!" Ken cried.

As soon as the chicks had disappeared the mother hen took wing, as wild and swift as a hawk. From far off toward the ocean beach came the strident warning of the cock.

The boys moved on once more, the two natives in the lead. Suddenly Matu drew up short. An exclamation escaped him. Judd and Ken, startled, halted likewise.

"Look!" cried Matu. "Look, American!"

The two boys followed Matu's forefinger. Ken saw only a pile of shell discolored with age and overgrown with tangle. But Judd dropped swiftly to his knees. He picked up a piece of the shell, his breath coming fast. It was black with exposure and dark with fungus, and the edges chipped off in his hand.

"What—what is it?" asked Ken, in a tight voice.

"It's black-lip," his friend murmured.

"Black-lip?"

Judd looked up and nodded, his eyes shining. "The most valuable pearl shell in the world!"

## CHAPTER VIII   SEA LOOT

S OMEONE HAS LOOKED for pearls here before!"
Ken's voice was hushed with awe. Matu and
Terii were as excited as children.

"It must have been years ago," Judd assured him.
"See how black and brittle the shell is. But let's scout
around—there may be some signs of who it was."

Farther back in the dense undergrowth they stumbled upon all that was left of a rude shelter: just a floor of coral shale with four rotted uprights overturned and all but decomposed by time and the elements.

"Golly! What's that?" Ken gripped his friend's arm.

"*Aué!*" exclaimed Matu in consternation.

The bleached bones of a skeleton gleamed whitely in the sand. Poking away the vines and creepers with his toe, Judd exposed the upper half of a skull. It grinned at him derisively and sent a cold shiver down his spine. "It's—it's the man who found the pearl shell, I guess."

"A lot of good it did him." Now Ken's scientific instinct came to the fore and he was examining the bones while Matu and Terii looked on in horror. Nothing could have persuaded the two natives to have touched that skeleton. Even to linger in its vicinity was ill luck. "Dead at least fifty years," Ken was saying. "Look at the ossification of this tibia. . . ."

Judd found the bone handle of a knife such as might have been used to open a pearl shell. The blade had long since corroded and rusted away. There was nothing else to indicate who this castaway might have been, nor to tell the manner of his death, surrounded there by his pile of precious shell.

"He may have been a deserter from that French surveying boat, the *St. Etienne,* who prospected here in 1888 according to Bergstrom."

"If he found any pearls there's no use looking for them in these sand dunes."

"No," Judd answered, "but we can look for them where he did—in the lagoon."

"Righto!"

The two boys hurried away from the grisly spot, to find that Matu and Terii had already fled to the beach.

"Let's start diving right now," cried Judd. "No telling when we'll have another chance. It won't take Matu long to find out what's on the bottom."

They clambered back into the canoe, filled with the excitement of their discovery.

"What kind of shell did you say that was, Judd?"

"Black-lip, as near as I could tell. Nothing like it for value! It's worth as much as pearls themselves."

"Phew! How do you suppose this shell escaped the castaways of the *Antipodes?*"

"Because shell's hard to see on the lagoon bottom by any except expert divers. Pearl oysters match their backgrounds; they become matted with barnacles and sea growths. The men probably didn't go diving around just for fun; they had one idea in their heads and that was escape."

"It's a lucky thing we've got Terii and Matu with us to dive."

The two native boys, usually so easy-going, were as nervous as race horses. It was always so with natives just before they began to dive.

From the Indian Ocean to the Persian Gulf, from Ceylon to Japan—wherever men dive for pearls—the Polynesian is conceded to be master of the art. Matu and Terii were no exceptions. In common with all boys of their race they had been born on the sea's very edge; they learned to splash and paddle before they learned to walk. And they had listened, ever since they could remember, to the old men telling tales of heroes who were great divers. As small boys they re- trieved shells from the shallows. As they grew older they progressed from one depth to another; their lungs developed; they learned the art of storing air. If their canoe upset they bailed it out, righted it, and climbed aboard again. Thus they became, by slow and logical degrees, almost amphibian; half men, half fish.

"Why do you say the shell is as valuable as the pearls?" Ken was asking.

"Because it's a commodity and not a luxury," his friend informed him. "They make all sorts of gadgets from it: buttons and knife handles and whatnot."

"And black-lip is rarer than any other kind?"

"There are only a few islands in the world, I believe, where it's found."

Matu brought the outrigger to a halt in eight fathoms. Peering over the side, they scanned the sea bottom eagerly.

"Maybe *you* can see shell," Ken complained. "But it all looks alike to me."

"Here, take the water glass." Judd handed him a boxlike contraption with a sheet of glass set into the bottom, enabling the observer to see to a great depth. Ken peered through it excitedly.

On their left hand a wall of coral descended to the floor of the lagoon, lost in submarine mystery. The sides of the coral cliff were marked by shadowy caverns, refuge for countless fishes. The sun beat down vindictively, lighting the water to an astonishing depth.

Matu adjusted his goggles and climbed over the gun-wale. He clung to the side, making strange whistling sounds as he inhaled and exhaled, his deep chest expanding. Then he released the air in a long, rasping breath. This preparation of the lungs is part of the ritual of every diver and is never slighted; the body must be prepared to withstand the pressure of the depths. Next, Terii handed him a basket that he had hurriedly plaited from palm leaves. He tied a stout line to the basket handle and lowered it to the bottom. Primarily, this basket was to be filled with such shell as Matu would wrest from the coral, but it served another purpose as well—the cord attached to the handle was Matu's only means of returning to the surface. When he wished to rise, he would begin his ascent hand over hand. If he should lose sight of his basket while working on the bottom he would be as good as gone.

Skin-diving—as it is called in the islands—is a precarious undertaking. In the Tuamotus, Judd had often been down to a depth of thirty or forty feet, but below that he had never ventured. It was a calling that took inevitable toll in the end; throughout the islands lie the wrecks of these divers, crippled in body, deaf, paralyzed by the "bends," or with limbs that have been amputated by sharks. The native's only weapon of defense against attack is a small sheath knife worn on a string around his neck.

"How about sharks, anyway?" Ken was asking anxiously. "Some of those we've seen lately haven't looked exactly friendly. Yet the natives don't seem scared of them."

"They're not scared of them," Judd assured him. "But don't think they don't hold 'em in wholesome respect! And barracudas, too. But they can see sharks and defend themselves if they have to. It's the *feké* that scares the life out of the native—and no wonder."

"The *feké*—what's that?"

"The giant octopus. Here in the atolls they run the largest in the world. They have a sort of protective mottling, and they can change color to match their background; they're almost impossible to see— until it's too late."

"I've heard that it's not been proved that sharks really do attack human beings," said Ken dubiously.

"I know," Judd nodded. "I've heard that, too."

"Then you believe they're wrong?"

For answer, Judd rolled up one leg of his white ducks. A scar stretched in a thin, jagged line across the calf of his leg.

"Golly! How'd you come by that?"

"When I was a kid, eight or nine. . . . I was

swimming with some natives in Fakarava, when someone cried, '*Ma'o!* Shark!' We all beat it for a rock—
the shark after us. I was one second too late. It was
only a small fellow, too; lucky for me."

"Say, I guess you'd better collect that standing reward from my Museum."

"A well-fed shark's usually harmless," Judd went
on, "but a hungry one's as dangerous as a wounded
buffalo, and don't you forget it! I've seen a tiger shark
tear the paddle from a native's hand, and sink its teeth
over and over into the bottom of a heavy canoe. How
long do you think a swimmer would have survived
in that water?"

"But those are only the big ones," Ken protested
weakly. "Out in deep water——"

"Don't you believe it! Once in Hikueru my dad
and I were watching some kids splashing in the shallows, when we heard a boy scream and begin to
thrash about. By the time we reached him the water
was full of blood. A tiger shark, scarcely three feet
long, had the kid by the arm. It kept up the attack
until Dad and I grabbed it by the tail and dragged it
to the beach, and it certainly was a handful."

"Say! What are you trying to do, scare the liver
out of me? Anything else to watch out for?"

"Only conger eels," Judd reassured him with a

grin. "They've got a head like a terrier's and they're great for hiding in crevices in the coral, watching for a fish, or a diver's ankle. . . . But you can always get away from them."

"How?—just in case I need to."

"Well, you wait quietly till the conger loosens his jaws to get a better grip. Then—a quick wrench and you're free. It's easy!"

Ken wiped the perspiration from his forehead with a limp hand. "I've never admitted it before, Judd, but do you know that I—I can't even swim?"

"*What?*" the other returned incredulously.

"It's a fact. Right now I'm scared silly this canoe will tip over and empty us out!"

In all his life Judd had never known a human being who couldn't swim. He could scarcely have been more astonished if Ken had told him that he couldn't walk, or sleep, or use his hands.

"I know it sounds childish," Ken admitted, "but the truth is I'm afraid of the water—just plain afraid! I suppose you're disgusted with me."

"Why no, but—but it seems to me like being scared of the wind, or the air."

With a few instructions to Terii, Matu placed between his toes a strong cord to which a heavy lump of coral had been attached. The native knew to within seconds just how long it would take him to regain the surface; he knew also that if he should fail to reach the air before his lungs were emptied, he would be unable to rise at all and would sink like a stone.

With a final deep breath, the boy gripped his nose with one hand and the cord with the other. Then he disappeared feet first in a cloud of bubbles. The three in the canoe looked over the side, watching the diminishing figure as it turned from brown to green to yellow.

Thirty feet down Matu released the weight and turned over, swimming with powerful strokes for the lagoon floor. Watching from above, Judd and Ken could see him clearly, moving through a fantastic sea world and apparently as much at home in it as if he had no need of air to breathe, or earth to stand upon; half boy, half fish, and doubtfully human.

Now they saw him working among the shells, quick-fingered; wrenching, cutting, filling his basket. Once in the Tuamotus Judd had seen Rotui, a famous diver, descend to a depth of one hundred and twenty feet, staying under for three minutes and twenty seconds. But that was phenomenal. The following year had found Rotui a victim of the bends—that dread affliction caused by coming from a high air pressure too suddenly to a lower one, bringing with it the characteristic cramping, or bending, which, if it doesn't kill its victim, leaves him permanently crippled.

For perhaps two and a half minutes Matu worked. Then he gave the signal for Terii to pull up the basket. Matu shot to the surface. He clung to the outrigger for a moment until his breathing returned to normal.

Judd's hands trembled as they examined the shell. Just as he had thought, it was the beautiful black-lip, what scientists call *margaritifera*—found most often in the atolls of the Tuamotus and the Gulf of California.

"Look at the size of this one!" he exclaimed. "It must be fifteen inches across!"

Five of them filled Matu's basket. They were the finest shells Judd had ever laid eye upon. His heart beat high with hope as he seized one of the shells and pried open its edges. He was well aware of the disappointments which can await the pearl fisher.

"It's a gambler's game, Ken," he said. "You never know. . . . You can open a thousand shell and not find so much as a 'seed'; and the next oyster may be filled with pearls of great value."

The first four shells yielded nothing—not even a seed. He opened the fifth shell and ran a skillful forefinger beneath the oyster's rim, and all of a sudden his heart gave a leap and started thumping. There, within the shell, blinking in the sunlight like an idol's eye, lay a black pearl of perfect symmetry and luster. It nestled in the cup of Judd's hand, glowing with living, ambient flame.

"*Aué! Te poé ravarava!*" breathed Terii.

"How much do you suppose it weighs?" Ken demanded excitedly.

Judd shook his head. "Don't get too optimistic," he warned. "We may never find another pearl; and certainly not another like this. But there's a tidy sum in the shell, anyway."

"But what good is it going to do us? We could hide pearls from Bergstrom, but you can't disguise a load of shell."

"At least we can dive for it, every chance we get, and leave it to rot out on the beach. Some day we may be able to do something about it."

"You mean—if we ever get home alive we might organize an expedition and come down here and reclaim the shell?"

"Something like that. Anyway, we'll keep quiet about it for the time being. I'll pledge Matu and Terii not to talk about it, even to the other Samoans. Secrets have a way of leaking out, and Bergstrom would never let us take a pearl out of this lagoon and live to tell the tale."

"That's right. How do you suppose the shell has escaped his notice?"

"It won't for long. He's had the wreck on his mind for one thing, and—as I told you—shell is hard for anyone but an expert to see. But you can be sure Tor Jansen will bring up the news with him as soon as he starts diving—if he hasn't noticed already."

"And then what?"

Judd shrugged. "Bergstrom will never leave this island while there's a possible pearl in the lagoon."

"Is there any reason why we shouldn't get what we can first?"

"No reason at all, my lad. Pearls belong to the man who finds them."

Within the next hour Matu and Terii made some ten dives each. The canoe was filling with the great shell. Then while the two youths rested, Judd decided to try his hand at diving himself. He hitched a *pareu* about his waist and slipped over the side. Matu handed him a basket and weight, while Terii hung the knife cord around his neck.

"Watch out for the *ma'o*," the youth grinned.

"And the *feké*," joked Terii.

Ken's face was drawn in anxious lines. This lagoon world was filled with mysteries that he, for one, felt no impulse to explore. He had never seemed to him-

self so utterly useless as he did in this moment. How
foolish were University degrees when you couldn't
even swim a stroke! He felt that he would willingly
have exchanged all his knowledge, all his degrees, for
a portion of the skill in the water which to these boys
was as natural as breathing.

Judd grinned back at them and began to breathe
deeply, forcing his diaphragm downward and pumping air into his lungs, like a compressor. Then holding
his nose, he descended feet first in a cloud of bubbles.
About twenty feet down he turned over and swam
rapidly for the bottom. Already the pressure on chest
and eardrums was great. A glance upward revealed
the dim shape of the canoe, drifting idly.

Sunlight filtered down into this green element in
long oblique rays, as if through the windows of some
submerged cathedral; cool bands of light, like floating
motes in the earth's dust—only here green, green. And
so little loss was there in its brightness that it seemed
to the boy as if he were suspended in mid-air above a
strange continent. Looking about him now, Judd
found himself in a garden of staghorn corals, their
branching antlers rising fifteen feet above his head.
Schools of jellyfish throbbed past, fish like opalescent
lamps in which the light was hardly yet extinct. He
saw tiny motes of filmy clouds which he knew to be

flying snails—delicate-pointed shells driven along by a pair of flapping wings. Gaudy parrot fishes browsed on the coral, looking at him with hard eyes; trigger fish swimming through a jungle of animal plants—plants which appeared to be dead stumps and skeletonized fronds, but which actually were living corals made by millions of tiny polyps concealed within their cubicles. There were silvery *tanurés;* brown-spotted *kitos;* square-nosed *tinga-tingas.* A cavern yawned at Judd's side, dark with mystery, and he moved hastily away from it, having no desire to explore its secrets. It seemed a lurking place of unimaginable horrors.

A dark shadow passed above his head and he glanced upward in alarm as a sand shark swam lazily by, its belly dull-gleaming in the cool light. It was necessary to walk carefully, for the reef was a honeycomb of holes and passages—haunt of the octopus, and of the man-eating rock cod, known as the *tonu;* while buried just below the surface of the sand lurked the dreadful *nohu,* the spines of whose dorsal fin were as hollow as the fangs of a rattlesnake and as filled with venom. A *totara,* or sea porcupine, blew itself up like a football at Judd's approach. The sandy floor was strewn with starfishes, miraculous to behold, and ugly sea slugs—the *bêche de mer.*

He had been under water for about a minute, and he knew that another minute would be his limit. He must hurry. Now he was among the shell beds. As he approached the pearl oysters, they snapped tight shut, seeming to feel the vibrations while he was still some distance away. Judd seized a shell, cut at its base, flipped it into his basket; then another, and yet another. His breath was almost gone. He knew that if he should remain under water too long he would collapse as he neared the surface, and then sink rapidly. He yanked the basket cord and sprang upward toward the light. He was sensible of the changing pressure as he passed swiftly to the surface. His head broke water and he clung to the side of the canoe, breathing deeply.

"*Mea maitai!* Good!" Matu nodded approvingly. "You did well, American. You have three shells."

"But you got five!"

The native laughed. "It is a game of children for us." Matu prepared to climb back into the water. "I saw a giant shell down there that I did not get last time. I shall bring it up with me now." He disappeared in a cloud of bubbles. The three boys watched him from above, following each movement as he worked far below among the shadowy shells.

Suddenly, without warning, they saw a whiplash

like section of hose shoot out from a coral cavern at
Matu's back. With the speed of light it encircled his
waist. In a split second another coil appeared, to twist
itself about the boy's chest. Judd caught the flash of
white vacuum cups that lined the undersurface of the
tentacles. An exclamation of horror burst from him.

Terii had seen simultaneously. "*Aué! Te feké!*" he
cried.

Matu was fighting desperately to free himself from
the coils of the octopus. Already one tentacle had
pinned his knife to his chest. In a flash Terii was over
the side of the boat. He clung for a second to the gunwale; his lungs expanded to receive a mighty draft of
air. Then he disappeared. The boys saw him swimming toward the bottom at great speed.

Hanging over the side of the canoe, they watched,
scarcely daring to breathe, a terrible dread in their
hearts. They saw that the octopus had come forth at
last to fight for its life. Against the coral they could
barely distinguish the mottled purplish globe of body,
the saucer-round eyes as baleful and fixed as fate.
They saw Terii's arm raise, knife in hand, to strike.
Then an inky liquid clouded the scene, shutting it off
from sight.

Agonizing seconds dragged into a minute. The minute passed. . . . Perspiration stood out on Judd's

brow. Matu had been under water almost three minutes. It was humanly impossible for him to last much longer. Judd sprang to his feet. Anything was better than sitting here, not knowing. He was over the side in an instant.

At that second there was a splash beside the canoe. A head appeared—Terii's head. The boys saw that he was dragging Matu to the surface.

"Quick, American," Terii gasped. "Help us!"

It was the work of a moment to have them both into the canoe. Matu fell senseless to the floor. Judd grabbed him under the armpits and bent him double over a thwart.

"He has swallowed much," panted Terii, fighting for breath. The boy's sides heaved; his eyes bulged in his head. "Empty him well. Three times I stabbed that devil—once in the eye—before he let go. *Apaka!* I will eat his heart!"

Matu was beginning to recover. He opened his eyes, gave a sickly grin. In a few moments he sat up, leaning back against the gunwale, his breathing slowly returning to normal. When Judd was sure that the native boy was no longer in danger, he looked once again through the water glass. The water had cleared. He could see the octopus lying like a collapsed balloon on the floor of the sea. With lines and hooks he and Terii fished it up into the boat. The tentacles would make good eating for the crew. But although Judd had eaten squid and small octopods ever since he was a child, he knew that he could not have swallowed one mouthful of this monster. One of the rubbery tentacles brushed against his bare ankle: its touch was deathly cold, and he shuddered. Terii seized his spear and plunged it again and again into the body of his enemy, shouting to the sky a pæan of thanks to the gods of the sea who had rendered him victorious.

"Guess we've had enough for one day," Judd decided. "We'll have to unload this shell. We may as well start rotting it out on the beach. Some day we may come back for it!"

It was dark by the time they came in sight of the *Island Queen*. A half-circle of moon was rising behind the rim of black palms; the stars stood on their heads in the lagoon, and from the outer ocean came the ceaseless rumble of the seas breaking against the barrier reef.

As the outrigger glided noiselessly under the brig's counter, Judd could see the glow of Bergstrom's cigarette against the darkness, and distinguish Malloy's shadowy form. Tor Jansen was standing by the rail as motionless as a graven image. The boys had killed a turtle and a few birds and they were laden with fresh food as they clambered over the rail.

The men rose from their deck chairs. Bergstrom held a lantern aloft, and it seemed to Judd that he peered with more than usual alertness into his face. "Well, Judd . . . what did you discover?"

"We explored a couple of the islets," the boy parried. "There's enough bananas, breadfruit, and coconuts to last for months. We didn't locate any fresh water, but there must be some, for we saw wild pigs and they couldn't live without it. Probably some brackish wells somewhere. We'll scout around again, next chance we get. Certainly we won't starve here."

"That's good news." Bergstrom was in the best of spirits. Even Red Malloy grunted approval at nature's beneficence.

Tor Jansen had not moved. The pearl that Matu had found was knotted into a handkerchief in Judd's pocket, but as the man's eyes ran over him it seemed to the boy that the pearl in his pocket was as big as an orange. He was thankful for the darkness which covered his confusion. He felt sure now that his life and Ken's were in great danger. When he had ceased to be useful to Bergstrom, the man would strike. Well, somehow, he, Judd Anders, would strike first!

## CHAPTER IX   TEN FATHOMS DEEP

Two weeks dragged by in fruitless search for the sunken specie; two weeks of ragged nerves and strained tempers. Day after day Red Malloy and Tor Jansen descended to the wreck of the *Antipodes* and searched about, ten fathoms deep in submarine gloom. Bergstrom paced the deck while the two divers were below, his face white and tense; and with each ascent to the surface, and each discouraging report, the Swede's temper became shorter and shorter, while the atmosphere aboard the *Island Queen* grew daily more taut.

In the meantime, while the two divers rested, the boys had had several days to themselves to put in as they wished. These days they spent at the pearl beds, ten miles south of the brig's anchorage. There Judd and Matu and Terii made many trips to the lagoon bottom, while Ken opened shell until his hands were raw and bloody, and their collection of "black-lip" grew to goodly proportions. A sizable pile of it lay rotting-out on the beach, though what they would do with it, or when they would ever be able to salvage it, remained a mystery.

The shell beds of Vana Vana had never been worked, and the high temperature of the water was ideal for propagation. The bottom of the lagoon seemed to have been designed for shell alone, since it was hard with coral, free from mud, and full of calcified algæ and shells. All nature had conspired to make this tiny atoll a perfect breeding ground for black-lip shell.

But the pearl harvest, as a matter of fact, proved to be disappointingly small. The boys found a fair number of seed pearls, of no value except in the

Orient, where pearls of irregular shape are used for jewelry. They found, too, several pearls of the variety known as *coq de perle:* imperfectly formed and attached to the inner shell. Pearls of the first water are, of course, extremely rare, since these must be perfect in form and color, free from flaw or blemish. But Matu had found one other to match the first one he had brought up. They were both black pearls bred of black-lip shell, worth possibly fifteen hundred dollars apiece.

In their impatience the boys felt that they had all too little time for their own activities, but they dared not spend too many hours away from the ship lest Bergstrom become suspicious and start investigating. Bergstrom was a driver, and only the limitations of physical endurance persuaded him to let Red Malloy and Tor Jansen rest from time to time. It was on these rare occasions that Judd and Ken were free to leave the brig. But they made each leisure hour count, and watched with satisfaction their pile of black-lip grow larger and larger. The two black pearls they packed in oakum and hid under a loose floor board in their cabin, together with their little store of "seeds."

Relations between the three partners had long been strained, and now it seemed that they had almost reached the snapping point. The memory of the morning when Malloy had chastised Tor Jansen marked a milestone in their relationship. It was evident to the whole ship's company that the little man had neither forgotten nor forgiven that humiliation; it ate like a corrosive into his soul. A plan must have begun to form at the back of his mind. . . .

But Red Malloy, indifferent now to Tor Jansen and Bergstrom alike, went ahead with his diving operations in the businesslike manner of a professional. Malloy may have tried, Judd thought, for some obscure reason of his own to have passed himself off as a seaman. But whatever his secret game might be, there was no doubt whatever as to the man's skill as a deep-sea diver. He knew what he was about.

"I tell you," he grumbled one morning, as he was preparing for the descent, "it looks like this whole job was a blasted hoax! I don't believe there *was* any gold on that blasted tramp, if you ask me."

"Nobody asked you," Bergstrom snapped back at him. "That gold's there all right and you two have got to find it."

"Goin' on two weeks we've been lookin', and where is it?" growled Malloy. "Ain't in the captain's cabin. Ain't in the purser's. Ain't in none of the other officers', neither."

"You were mate on the *Antipodes*, Malloy—how

could they have stowed all that specie without you knowing it?"

" 'Aven't I already told you, Axel," the other returned, with a cold, deadly patience. "That gold was stowed afore any of the crew or officers come aboard. Only one man knew where that gold was—Captain Wilderson; and I guess he won't tell."

"Kassel said that you knew."

" 'E's balmy in the crumpet."

"Well—where are you going to search next?"

"Jansen's workin' the galley. I'm goin' over the saloon with a fine-tooth comb."

"If it isn't there, the sooner you two start on the engine room the better!"

"Bli'me!" Malloy exploded wrathfully. "Who do you think you're talkin' to? If anybody 'as a 'ankerin' for my job it's theirs and welcome." His chin shot out in the belligerent thrust that the boys had come to recognize. The two men looked at one another with hard eyes and clenched fists. For a moment battle trembled in the air. Then the Swede's eyes dropped. Bergstrom swung silently on his heel and walked for'ard along the deck, where Tor Jansen was attending to his own gear. The two boys watched this passage at arms with interest. They wondered what the final spark would be that would touch off the explosion.

"If I was Malloy I wouldn't care much about diving with Jansen," Judd observed. "It's too easy for accidents to happen under water. He hates Malloy—no doubt about that." The boy was looking for'ard with interest as Bergstrom helped his crony into the clumsy suit. The little man writhed and struggled as the heavy folds settled over his meager frame. The weighty suit seemed to incase the little figure like the skin of a prehistoric creature, half bird and half beast. "Could anything make a man look more like a monster than one of those suits?" the boy queried.

"I'll bet," Ken said, in his best professional manner, "that you don't know the history of the diving suit."

"Lord! I'll bet I don't either."

Ken frowned solemnly down his nose with the air of classroom owlishness that was one of his most engaging traits. "The diving suit as we know it today, my son, is about one hundred years old. It was in 1830 that August Siebe invented the 'closed' suit that made underwater work possible."

"That so?" Judd sniffed. "What else do you know about it, Professor?"

"Hmmm! Your thirst for knowledge is gratifying. To continue—Aristotle speaks of a diving bell used by the Greeks two thousand years ago. And—er—that's about all," he finished lamely.

"So what!" scoffed Judd.

Matu and Terii were dragging the pumps into place and clearing the decks for the business of the day. Tor Jansen's air tanks were set up on the fo'c'sle head; Malloy's amidships.

Red Malloy's equipment consisted of two complete sets: steel tanks, three feet by ten, strong enough to stand an air pressure of one hundred and twenty-five pounds, with a two-hundred-pound pressure gauge connected to a diving manifold. There were two copper helmets with non-return valves screwed fast, and six fifty-foot sections of air hose to form a connecting link between pump and diver. It was an outlay that represented considerable money, and it occurred to Judd that Red Malloy must have been a more than ordinarily successful "blackbirder" in the Solomons. Now that that nefarious trade had been outlawed, the man was turning his hand to another lucrative calling.

Judd and Ken found Malloy examining his gear with more than ordinary care. He looked up at the boys with a quizzical gleam in his little eyes.

"Take a squint at this, me 'earties," he invited, holding out a length of air hose for their inspection.

They examined it, and saw nothing out of the ordinary. The tubing was over an inch in diameter, with a bore of only half an inch; the hose was made up of three layers of processed rubber with two layers of fine linen between.

"Well, what about it?" Judd asked.

Malloy chuckled. "Guaranteed to stand a pressure of five 'undred pounds to the square inch," he said. "But this 'ere section wouldn't 'old ten pounds! It was all right yesterday, too."

Judd looked again, and now he could see that the outer layer had been split and very neatly mended. The four inner layers had been cut away and scraped. It appeared perfect to the unknowing eye.

"A reg'lar diver-killer," Malloy muttered.

Judd was startled. "You don't think——" he began, knowing the Samoans' dislike of the man.

Malloy shook his head. "Only a real diver could 'ave done this job; one familiar with 'ose and such. Kind o' looks like some bloke don't want me to come up alive. I wonder 'oo it could be?" His tongue went into his cheek.

"But there's only one real diver aboard besides yourself," Ken put in, "and that's——"

"You're a smart lad, Professor," Malloy interrupted him. "Shows what a college education will do fer a man. Now tike me—I never 'ad no schoolin' to speak of, but I do know a mended 'ose from a 'orse's neck.

Bli'me! I'd rather discover it on top than a 'undred feet down."

"What are you going to do about it?" Judd demanded.

"Do abaht it? Why, mend the 'ose, of course; and keep my trap shut and my glims open. Red Malloy didn't come down in the last rainstorm, not 'alf."

"But——" Ken began.

"Look, Professor: the surest way to 'and yerself over to yer enemy is to let 'im know you're watchin' 'im. You'll never catch 'im off guard that way. The Dummy's got it in fer me ever since that day I shook 'im up a bit. Blast me, I wish I'd popped the bleeder overboard and been done with it."

The two boys watched as he expertly repaired the section of hose. "There! Guess I'll keep my gear under padlock after this," he grumbled. "Say—look-a 'ere! I know you two ain't been exactly friendly toward me since I come aboard, and I don't know as I blime you much. I'm a 'ard man and I've lived a 'ard life. But I ain't a bad sort of blighter at 'eart. What you got against me, personal?"

"I guess it's only——" Judd hesitated.

"Crikey! I know without yer sayin' it. It's the company I keep, now ain't it? Well—let's stow all that. Misfortune leads a man into strange ways. . . . The missus always said that I took to wrong-doin' like a flea to a dog's ear, but that's an exaggeration. Just you lend me a 'and while I'm divin', will ye? I ain't 'ankerin' to park my bones in the 'old of the *Antipodes*."

"What do you want me to do?" Judd asked.

"Keep an eye on my air supply while I'm under. Them ruddy blacks ain't no good at it. It's a wonder I'm still alive with Ranga at the pumps these last two weeks. Keep an eye to the pressure and see that the gauges are right. I'm fond o' breathin'."

"You're going down now?"

"As soon as I fix this 'ere 'ose."

"Where do you think the gold is?"

Malloy gave him his foxy smile. "I've got a pretty good 'unch. Woke up with it this mornin'!"

"Where's that?" Judd persisted.

"That, my lad, would be tellin'; and what you don't know won't 'urt ye, savvy?" But there was no longer malice in his tone; almost it seemed as if there were a note of anxiety.

"I'll keep an eye on things while you're below," Judd heard himself answer. "But watch out, Malloy——"

Up by the for'ard boom Tor Jansen was preparing for his descent. Axel Bergstrom stood at his side, holding the copper helmet, testing the pressure in the air tanks. The little man presented an unbelievably grotesque figure in his diving suit. His small head with its pinched features and batlike ears protruded above the bulky collar, giving him something of the look of a child's toy. His meager body was concealed, but the cumbersome suit accented the octopal suggestion of his every motion. Before the copper helmet settled down over his shoulders, Tor Jansen looked aft at Red Malloy. Judd intercepted the look, and so filled with venom was it that it sent a shiver down the boy's spine. He found himself suddenly and unaccountably concerned for Malloy. The man was a scoundrel by his own admission, and yet there was something about him which made it impossible utterly to dislike him.

"Watch out, Malloy," Judd cautioned him once again. "I'd never turn my back on that fellow—under water or above."

Malloy laughed shortly. " 'Im?" he said scornfully. "I don't 'old no fear of 'im, not 'alf!"

"Nevertheless——"

"Forget all that, m'lad, and listen to what I'm tellin' you: you keep yer glims on the air 'ose, see? And pull in the slack before you do any signalin'. If you watch the bubbles you can tell where I am; and keep an eye on the measure line on the air 'ose, so's you can see 'ow much pressure I need; and always keep a safe margin of fifteen pounds in the tank, savvy?"

"Yes—but what are your signals?"

Malloy grinned. "Now don't get nervous. I've only got two signals and they're easy to remember: one pull on the lifeline means 'lower away, more air 'ose.' Two pulls means ' 'aul me up!' And when you get those two pulls, see that you 'aul me up and quick abaht it, for I'll be in a bleedin' 'urry. Nar then, nar then——"

He slipped into the cumbersome suit and stood upright while Judd fitted the breastplate and buckled on the leaden-soled shoes. Then he strapped on the hundred-pound belt and made sure that the diver's knife was firmly fastened in its sheath. Judd set the helmet on top of the breastplate and locked it with a quarter-turn. Malloy was overside, reaching for the descending line. Air rushed into the copper globe; with one hand the man clung for a second to the rope, while the other hand opened up the escape valve in his helmet. He hung there, adjusting his weight to the buoyancy of the air in his suit, while he tested out the valves. Then he looked along the foredeck where Tor Jansen had been preparing for his descent; but the grotesque figure had already disappeared, and Bergstrom was crouched over his air tanks.

Red Malloy wrapped his legs around the descending line and waved good-by to Judd and Ken, then started his descent. The two boys watched the bulky figure as it moved slowly, deeper and deeper, changing from yellow to green to blue. Then it vanished in the mystery of the shadowy wreck. Only occasional bubbles escaping from the air valves told them that Malloy still lived and had being in that fantastic world below the sea.

The deep-sea diver's greatest enemy is pressure. With every foot that he descends into the water this pressure increases. If he makes a dive of three hundred feet, there is a pressure of one hundred and thirty-three pounds upon every square inch of his body. Much less than that would be sufficient to crush him. However, as he descends, an air-valve control enables him to regulate his air supply so that the pressure in his helmet is a little greater than that of the water surrounding it. He is breathing this high-pressure air, and within his own body the pressure must be built up to resist that one hundred and thirty-three-pound push.

As the diver ascends to the surface, the pressure on the outside of his body decreases; the process of equalization is reversed. The blood carries the nitrogen away from his tissues and out through his lungs. If he ascends too rapidly, the gas will expand in bubbles in his tissues, causing permanent injury or death. The man at the pumps must be onto his job.

Judd, watching Red Malloy's pressure tank, felt unaccountably nervous. Seconds dragged into minutes. A quarter of an hour passed. Half an hour. Three quarters. . . . Somehow the figure of Tor Jansen haunted the boy and he could not shake off a feeling of oppression. Sooner or later the little man would square accounts with his enemy, and what better place to do so than under water, where a crime could so easily be made to seem an accident? If Malloy hadn't noticed the damaged air hose that morning, he would have been dead by this time. There were no limits to which the strange, twisted nature of Tor Jansen might drive him. Still, Malloy was no fool. He had lived a hard life, laughed at it and survived it: so Judd tried to reassure himself.

"Say, how long has he been under?" Ken was asking anxiously.

"Fifty minutes."

"How far down is he?"

"Seventy feet."

"What's the time-limit at that depth?"

"An hour, I'd say."

"There are still plenty of bubbles coming up. I guess he's all right."

"Yes. . . . *Wait! The bubbles have stopped!*"

At that moment Bergstrom's voice cried out in alarm and Matu was running swiftly to the Swede's side. As Judd looked up, he felt two sharp tugs on Malloy's lifeline. Two tugs. . . .

"Quick, Judd! Malloy's signaling!" cried Ken.

"Help me," the boy panted. "Lay hold! Something's happened!"

They pulled with all their strength. Up for'ard, Bergstrom and Matu were hauling in Tor Jansen's lifeline. It was with a feeling of utter relief that Judd saw Malloy's copper helmet break water, caught a glimpse of the man's face through the glass. He and Ken hauled Malloy on board. Judd's fingers seemed all thumbs as he unscrewed the globe. Malloy could hardly stand; he staggered, then sat down abruptly. His eyes were bloodshot. His hands sought his throat, as if he could never fill his lungs with enough air. The air hose dangled limply. Judd pulled it up. It had been cut through.

At that moment Tor Jansen was dragged aboard. Bergstrom caught at his clumsy figure and it slipped through his arms and collapsed on the deck like a deflated balloon. Bergstrom seized the air hose; it, too, had been sliced in half.

"You've killed him!" Bergstrom shouted at Malloy. "By God, I'll——" He leaped forward.

Malloy's breath had returned. "Take it easy, Axel,"

he rasped. "And take a squint at this." He held up his own severed air hose. " 'E thought 'e'd get me, the blighter! Well, I got 'im first."

"What do you mean?" The Swede's voice was deadly cold. He controlled himself with difficulty. The boys crowded around, scarcely daring to breathe.

"When I got down there," Malloy was saying, "The Dummy wasn't nowhere in sight. I 'ad a 'unch where that gold was; just a 'unch that I woke up with this mornin'. Down in the engine room was a row of steel lockers, big ones, that they use for tools and spare parts and such; and it occurred to me . . ."

"Go on!" Bergstrom ripped.

"I 'ad quite a job gettin' the lock busted on the first one, and I was afraid my air 'ose would get fouled. But the locks was pretty well rusted and I finally busted it with my bar."

"Well—I'm waiting, Malloy." The Swede was as taut as an arrow drawn.

"Let me breathe a second, man. . . ." Red Malloy, still pale, gulped down a deep breath. The circle around him watched, silent, hanging upon every word as it fell. "Meantime," Malloy suggested, pointing to the still figure on the deck, "you'd better cut 'im out o' that suit. Won't do no good, but won't do no 'arm, neither; and seems more respectful to the dead."

"Go on!" Bergstrom shouted, now losing all control, "or I'll——"

"Well, there wasn't nothin' in that first locker but cotton waste. When I opened the second locker it appeared like it was filled up with the same; but when I jabbed it with my bar, I felt somethin' 'ard. And there was a wooden box, all bound round with iron. Every locker was filled with boxes just like it, and I 'ave no doubt the words Bank o' Singapore is stenciled on every one."

Bergstrom's breath came fast. He had forgotten Tor Jansen. There was but one thought sweeping through his mind: the gold had been found. *Gold!* Fortune lay within the reach of his hands.

"I dragged several of the cases out on the floor of the engine room," Malloy was saying. "No weight to 'em at that depth. Then I saw The Dummy, and I motioned to 'im that the gold was found. I didn't think nothin' abaht it when 'e just stood there in the doorway with 'is blinkin' knife in 'and, for I'd seen a shark cruisin' around meself. But as I started toward the doorway—I 'ad been under nigh an hour by that time—I saw the blighter deliberately reach up and cut my air 'ose!"

An exclamation broke from Judd, but Bergstrom silenced him with a fierce gesture.

"I thought fast," Malloy said. "I grabbed the air 'ose below the cut and doubled it up tight, else I'd 'ave drowned standin' up. There was still air in my 'elmet, enough for another minute or so. Knowin' that, I felt calm-like. That's when I gave two tugs on my lifeline. But before I could be 'auled up, there was Jansen still standin' in the doorway, waitin' for me. I 'ad to get by 'im before I could rise. But I could move faster than 'e could now, because I'd no hose trailin' round be'ind me. I took out my sea knife and moved over to the door. He made a lunge for me and I dropped down at 'is feet. 'E passed right over me and I was out that door in a second. 'E turned about——

"I was getting dizzy by this time and I couldn't see much count o' my breath foggin' over the glass—but I knew 'e still 'ad all the air in the world and 'e was layin' for me. Unless I got 'im before 'e got me I'd be as 'elpless as a 'ooked fish. As I come up under his air 'ose I slashed at it with my knife. A clean cut. 'E never seemed to think of doublin' up 'is tube, like I done. The water must 'ave rushed into 'is bleedin' 'elmet and drowned 'im standin' up. 'E died, just as 'e 'ad planned for me. The *scut!*"

Silence fell over the little group of men, a chill silence that struck them to the marrow. It seemed minutes before anyone moved. Then Bergstrom knelt and unscrewed Tor Jansen's helmet with hands that were curiously gentle. The gnomish little figure lay piteous and inert; its eyes wide open and staring. Behind the eyes were phantoms of another world forever lost. . . .

At sunset a lifeboat rowed by Matu and Falé eased out through the reef passage into the open ocean. Judd was at the steering-sweep. Bergstrom sat hunched in the sternsheets. The swells of the ocean lifted and fell in gentle monotony; the palm trees held their breath. A canvas-wrapped bundle, singularly small and bound about with hemp, lay full length in the center of the boat. The reef muttered in its sleep. Overhead, the sky was red with the blood of titans; a world was dying and in flames. The fiery sun sank into the sea while a darkness almost palpable rose from the surface of the water. In spite of the warmth of the air Judd shivered. There was something indescribably desolate about the scene: the lonely expanse of ocean, the wide and oppressive sky; the canvas bundle so meager and forlorn. This was not the honest, decent burial of a man who had reached the end of his allotted span; there was something terrible and lost about it. Gulls followed the lifeboat croaking, croaking. . . .

The two Samoans, refusing to touch the dead, looked on in awed silence as Judd and Bergstrom lowered the bundle overside. The Swede's face was paper-white and his hands shook nervelessly. The waters parted with a soft hiss. . . . There was a flag tucked under the rope of the canvas wrapping. As the dark waters closed in, the flag came loose, floated for a moment in bold relief against the sea before it sank forever. Judd strained forward with startled eyes. That flag. . . . It bore a black cross on a white field, with the tricolor and the Maltese Cross in the corner. And then he knew. It was the war ensign of old Imperial Germany.

## CHAPTER X  LIGHT IN DARK PLACES

J UDD BOLTED his dinner and came up on deck for
a quiet hour before turning in. The cabin below
decks shut him in and he couldn't breathe; there was
something indescribably oppressive about it that laid
a heavy hand upon his spirit. Or perhaps it was the
tragedy of the day that he could not shake off, and
which invaded all his thoughts. Try as he would he

could not free his mind of the picture of that small, canvas-wrapped figure consigned to the deep. The boy paused by the shrouds, grateful for the freshness of the air that blew across the lagoon from the dew-laden *motus*. Ken was down in the cabin going over his interminable notes, sorting, filing, arranging. . . . Bergstrom was closeted with Malloy in mysterious conference, and the low hum of the two men's voices issued through the open skylight of the afterdeck.

The gold of the *Antipodes*—what ill fortune it had brought to all who had been concerned with it! Of the eighteen men who had sailed from New Zealand twenty-five years ago, only one of them—Red Malloy —was living to tell the tale. Judd thought of Karl Kassel, gone—perhaps shot down on the decks of the *Island Queen*. . . . What part had Kassel played in all this? And now Tor Jansen himself was buried beneath the sea, his tortured spirit stilled forever. Who had he really been? And Red Malloy himself—the man was playing some deep game of his own, but what was it?

The answers to these questions eluded the boy and deepened his sense of unease. He had a feeling that events were marching swiftly toward their inevitable conclusion; that he stood on the brink of some dark discovery. He tried to shake off the feeling but it persisted.

The ship lay quiet. The tide was on the ebb and the boy could almost feel the soft pull of it. These tides under the equator—ebbing and flowing with unchanging regularity, not varying in time from year's end to year's end. Full tide at midnight and noon, the ebb at six o'clock, morning and evening. You could set your watch by it.

Tonight Judd felt the smell of the sea all about him; that nameless odor with a subtle stimulant at the heart of it. Silence and mystery shrouded the dark circle of the lagoon. Overhead, the Milky Way spanned the sky like a triumphal arch to heaven, while the stars lay tracks of fire in the black waters of the lagoon. The boy welcomed the constellations as old, familiar friends. They reassured him with a sense of their certainty. He had sailed by them, slept under them, listened to legends about them ever since he could remember. He found his eye roving among them, as one who seeks a familiar face in an alien crowd. He discovered the Pleiades—called by the natives, with nice fancy, *Mataiki:* Little Eyes. And there was Scorpion: the Fish Hook of Maui. . . . He saw the rising of the Southern Cross, and off to the south the stardust streamers of the Magellan Clouds.

From the outer ocean came the muffled song of the surf, an ever recurring motif of melancholy in the symphony of the sea: a whispering hum of sound, like something heard in a shell. It was a sound that Judd would have been conscious of only if it had ceased. The cry of the questing gulls mingled with sea sounds, haunting the mind like the wail of uneasy ghosts, always complaining, never at rest.

The Samoans were lounging by the main hatch, the glow of their pandanus cigarettes dotting the darkness like fireflies. Their low voices and musical tongue reached Judd's ear, and he found himself half listening to their speech—more to its sound than to its sense. They were speaking of Tor the Silent One, and his lonely burial. Awe shadowed Matu's tones as he spoke of the *tupapau*—the ghost—that he most feared. It appeared in the form of a robber crab whose great legs were as long as the outrigger of a war canoe. It could have picked him up as easily as a man could pick up a baby. Once it had walked right over his head without touching him, but its breath was cold and of a terrible chill. Of course it was really the *tupapau* of his brother, who had been drowned at full-of-the-moon; for always the *tupapau* returned when the moon was bright, never in dark of night.

Three times had Matu encountered this ghost, and each time he had been so badly frightened that he fell to the ground, incapable of movement.

The voices of the natives droned on. . . . They spoke of the Lizard Men—the *Manahuné*—said to have been in possession of all the islands when the eyes of the first Polynesian voyagers glimpsed the peaks of Tahiti rising from the sea. Tales of the *Varua Ino:* the Spirit of Evil that dogs the footsteps of the living and preys upon the souls of the newly dead. Tales such as these had colored the background of their childhood as they listened, half waking, half sleeping, around the evening circle. Matu lit a match to dry a leaf of black tobacco over the flame, then he twisted it in a strip of pandanus and deeply inhaled the smoke.

The vagrant breeze fanned Judd's cheek as he leaned there against the rail. And standing there in the darkness, the boy was struck anew by the miracle of this island world. The romance of coral, still to be told, still fully to be understood. Vana Vana—all atolls—alive, growing. Fragile creatures those coral polyps, multiplying by billions on the sea floor, erecting castle walls of limestone which rise from no matter what great depth to the surface of the sea; dying almost at once in sunlight and air. But the lower cells of the massive reefs are filled with living animals. Attacked by the sea, devoured by fishes, they heal every wound out of their own substance. Always dying, always being reborn. Every atoll, every reef, an organic whole—a thing alive. Thousands upon thousands of miles of them scattered throughout the equatorial waters of the sphere—it was a thought to stagger the mind.

And the undersea world—almost as unknown as that of Mars or Venus; a world which had yielded up but few of its secrets. Judd's mind stirred at the thought of that vast submarine continent, as the marvelous life forms beneath the ocean have stirred the imaginations of men since first the Phoenicians dared to sail the open sea. The lower depths, home of the *feké*; of the giant clam whose shells are sometimes five feet long, with valves that close like a wolf-trap upon the hand of any diver luckless enough to touch them. What unknown wonders moved and had their being there in submarine darkness? The luminous fishes: galaxies, constellations, meteors under the sea. And the Pacific "high" islands: were they, as some believed, only the mountain peaks of a submerged continent which stretched its broken back from Asia to Peru? What of the unsolved riddle of Easter Island, whose mammoth stone idols stand with their backs to the sea, their origin shrouded in the mystery of time?

Often Judd had lost himself in such fancies, sensible of the mysteries of this island world in which he had been born. But tonight he found no comfort in this familiar world. The tragedy of the day had left him restive and ill at ease. He thought of Mata Afa, and of Man Who Laughs; of Ghost Girl, and the fragrant valleys of Tahiti. And so unreal did that old life seem that he had consciously to summon up what those people said or did, what they ate, what sort of clothing they wore. They seemed to belong to the realm of imagination; a fading afterglow in his memory.

As he stood there, lost in thought, he was aware of an alien sound crossing his consciousness: Bergstrom's voice. The man's tongue had loosened with alcohol and his voice carried clearly now up through the open skylight. The glow of the swinging lamp in the room below made a square of warmth in the darkness. The Swede and Red Malloy were closeted in secret conference. . . . What were they talking about? What dubious plan were they hatching now?

Judd moved silently across the deck and looked down through the skylight. He could see Bergstrom and Malloy sitting across from each other at the green-topped table, the same table where Judd had sat

that night they fled from Tahiti. It was apparent that
the discovery of the specie and the success of the expedition had ironed out the differences between the
two men, at least upon the surface. If Bergstrom har-
bored blame against his confederate for Tor Jansen's
death there was no evidence of it in his manner. He
poured himself a jorum of rum and held the glass up
to the light, relishing its amber glow. A slight smile
played about his thin, cold lips.

"What's on yer mind, Axel?" Malloy was asking.
"You've been chin-wagging for 'alf an hour and you
'aven't said a thing. You 'aven't forgotten that I'm in
on this deal, too, 'ave you?"

Bergstrom allowed a smile to drift over his pale
face, but he made no answer as he sipped his rum.

Malloy leaned swiftly across the table and said,
without raising his voice: "You wouldn't be thinkin'
of double-crossin' me, would you, Axel?" His laugh
came short and sharp. "Because it wouldn't be
'ealthy, my friend."

Bergstrom's face was devoid of expression as he answered: "You ought to know me better than that,
Malloy. I've never yet let down a friend."

"That so?" the other returned. "What abaht Karl
Kassel, then?"

"I had nothing to do with that. There was trouble

between Tor Jansen and Kassel from the very first. I tried to keep things smooth between them, and tried to get it into Tor's head that without Kassel our hands were tied. But it didn't do any good. He flew into one of his rages one day and shot Kassel. He was sorry about it afterwards."

Up on deck Judd caught his breath. So his and Ken's suspicions had been correct. Kassel *had* been shot.

"Was he, now?" Malloy was murmuring in mock sympathy.

Bergstrom shrugged the subject aside and spoke of that which lay closest to his interest. "How long do you think it will take you to bring up the gold?" The glass that he lifted to his lips trembled now, and streaks of amber light shifted across the table.

"About three days, I'd say. Maybe four. There are forty boxes, and ten dives a day is plenty fer Red Malloy."

"Couldn't Anders help?"

" 'E'd be no 'elp at that depth. And after the gold's stowed—what next?"

Bergstrom laughed softly. "Simple as child's play! We weigh anchor for Singapore. I've friends in China. I'll have no trouble cashing in the gold. And with all that money, the world's our oyster."

"But the Samoans," Malloy reminded him. "They've got tongues in their 'eads, 'aven't they? 'Ow are you going to shut them up?"

Bergstrom smiled thinly, and sipped his rum. "Haven't you forgotten what you brought your head-hunters along for, my friend? Six of them ought to be able to take care of five Samoans."

"Mmmm! And the two boys—they're not bad blokes. I'm 'alf fond of them. What about them?"

The fingers that held the cigarette were now quite steady. Bergstrom's voice was deadly cold as he answered: "We need Judd Anders to get us to the China coast, my friend. But once in sight of land—well, the sea keeps its secrets. . . ."

"Oho! So that's it," Malloy chuckled. "If you ain't a devil with two sets o' horns, then I'm a ruddy Dutchman, Axel."

The Swede laughed. "Perhaps that's why we get along so well, Malloy."

Judd moved cautiously away from the skylight. Now he knew what to expect and when to expect it. Once in sight of the China coast . . . His heart hardened and he clenched his fists. The utter callousness with which Bergstrom planned to dispose of him and Ken and the five Samoans filled him with horror. And as for Red Malloy, lending his approbation to the scheme—— It was a pity Tor Jansen hadn't succeeded when he cut Malloy's air hose. Drowning would have been too good for the scoundrel! There was no choice between either of them.

He went below to tell Ken the fateful news.

## CHAPTER XI   THUNDER ON THE REEF

THE NEXT THREE DAYS passed by in unremitting activity. One by one the boxes of specie were hauled up from the lagoon floor. One by one, until there were forty in all: trim boxes bound about with rusty iron bands, and the words once neatly stenciled on their sides but now almost indecipherable: *Bank of Singapore*. Harmless-looking boxes to have caused so much death and destruction.

Malloy was exhausted with the stupendous, solitary effort of all that diving. A constitution less tough than his own would have cracked under the strain, and Judd marveled at the man's sinewy endurance. Even now the boy could not explain, even to himself, just how he felt toward Red Malloy. He knew the man to be an utter blackguard, knew him to be lending passive if not active support to Bergstrom's future schemes. And yet there was a toughness of fiber about the man that commanded his grudging respect. Perhaps under more fortunate circumstances Malloy would have followed a different path.

When all the boxes had been stowed against the wall in Bergstrom's cabin, the Swede in high good spirits granted the men a two-days' rest before weighing anchor for Singapore. They all needed it. The Samoans were worn out with their concentrated labors; now they were content just to lie about the decks, eating and sleeping away the hours.

But the Solomon Islanders, who had never been allowed ashore, took full advantage of this opportunity for freedom. They unlashed their high-stemmed canoes from the fo'c'sle head, set the outriggers in place, and prepared to visit the nearest *motu*. There they would hunt the wild pig and gorge themselves upon fresh food. They chattered like excited apes. Theirs had been a hard lot aboard the *Island Queen*. To keep them out of mischief and prevent trouble with the Samoans, Judd had seen to it that the blacks had never a waking moment to themselves. To them Judd Anders was a white devil whose powers of invention were without bounds. The black canoes swing overside to the accompaniment of a rousing savage chant, and soon their paddles flashed in unison as they left the side of the brig.

The stillness of early morning rested upon land and lagoon. There was no stir in the green mystery of the encircling *motus*; the palms held their heads quite still, as if they were listening for the familiar voice of the sea.

"Can't we do some exploring?" Ken asked his friend. "After all, I don't want to write a monograph on deep-sea diving. There may be some ruins on one of those *motus* and I'd like to find out."

"Righto!" Judd agreed with enthusiasm. "It'll be good to get off this ship and stretch our legs; it's going to be a long ride to Singapore! We'll take Matu and Terii along with us."

Their canoe swung away from the brig and Matu ran up the sail. A breeze was blowing fresh and steady from the quarter of the rising sun, ruffling the lagoon over the shoal patches and stirring the dark fronds of the palms. Judd glanced back at the *Island Queen*, riding so trimly to her anchor. Her spars glistened in the sun and the paint of her hull gleamed sharp and white against the water. The Solomon Islanders had done their allotted work well, albeit unwillingly: the brig was in the pink of condition. Matu let the sheet out and leaned back with both hands on the steering paddle, holding the sheet with his foot. The canoe gathered way and seemed fairly to leap through the water. As they rounded the point and lost sight of the *Island Queen*, their course lay straight across the lagoon to the southernmost *motu*, ten miles distant. They were moving through a channel where the water deepened in color. A school of porpoises appeared suddenly, playing back and forth across the path of the canoe, so close at times that Matu could have touched them with his paddle, and their breathing was clearly audible as they broke the surface.

They vanished as mysteriously as they appeared, and a few moments later they were seen moving northward, far across the lagoon.

In something less than an hour the nose of the canoe slid up on the beach and the boys sprang ashore. The *motu*, perhaps half a mile long and two hundred yards deep, rose from the shallows on the inner side of the reef. The white coral shingle, against which the waters of the lagoon lapped gently, presented a blazing foreground for the dense foliage. A path made by wild pigs led through the jungle across the island to the ocean beach. Down this trail the four boys started. Hermit crabs scurried away at their approach, dragging their shell houses into the shade of the scrub. Gannets and ghost terns wheeled and skimmed above the palms. It was indescribably remote, touched by a sense of isolation that not even the Samoans' high-spirited laughter served to dispel; a paradise for small boys to play pirate and castaway.

Many times, wool-gathering over his books, Ken Henderson had imagined wandering down the beach of just such a tropic isle as this, with a tawny crew at his heels, searching for a loot of specie and pearls. Tales of the equatorial islands had charmed his childhood; he had forgotten them, lost them somewhere in the schoolroom. But now, chance-led, he had discovered that their fine reality far exceeded childish imagining. How unreal those long scholarly years of scientific research now seemed! Here he felt alive, as if he were standing on the threshold of experience and eager venture. He had come to Tahiti to round out his studies in Polynesian ethnology, and the old habits of mind died hard. But he had discovered the deep satisfaction of living with the sun, of hearing the thunder of the reef in his ears. He knew with his mind that those years of study had not been wasted, that they had been rich in accomplishment. And yet at this moment he would gladly have traded it all for a tithe of Matu's swift, wild strength, or Judd's self-assurance on the sea. "Why," Ken thought wryly, "I can't even swim. I'm scared of the water!"

Terii was in the lead. He drew up with an exclamation and motioned to the others to halt.

"*Puaa!* Wild pig!" came the native's sibilant whisper.

The boys saw it then, half hidden in the jungle. The pig's black head was lowered, tusks gleaming, waiting. . . .

The blade of Terii's machete was twenty inches long, bright with death. The youth took a firm grip on its handle, drew a deep breath and shouted a loud-voiced challenge. As if awaiting that challenge, the

boar charged. Flecks of foam flew back from its jaws.
Judd could see the curled tusks, the wicked eyes.
Straight for them, it tore over the ground with a
grunting snort.

Terii met the charge with a perfectly timed thrust.
The animal impaled itself on the knife, hilt-deep. A
shiver ran through its black body. It rolled over on its
side, lay still.

The two natives shouted with joy, trussed up the
animal's feet with stout vines and slung it over a pole.

"*Aué te aué!*" Matu crowed gleefully. "Now we'll

MATU
AND
TERII

have a *tamaaraa*—a feast. Pig roasted in the *umu*. Ho!
Ha!"

Down the trail they all but ran, the pig swinging on
a pole suspended between the two Samoans' shoulders.
As they emerged from the jungle on the ocean side of
the atoll, the beach seemed to stretch away on either
hand for an immeasurable distance. It sloped down
sharply to ramparts of broken corals, and out beyond
that lay the barrier reef, where scattered rock pools
held patches of water that looked like fragments of
fallen sky. Farther out still, waves rose and fell in
glassy splendor.

While Terii cleaned the pig at the sea's edge, Matu
set about making the *umu:* the native oven. First he
started a roaring fire and threw into it a large pile of
stones, to be heated through. Next he scooped out a
wide, deep hollow in the ground and filled it with
leaves. Terii brought up the pig. By this time the
stones were red-hot and the animal was filled with
them. Then the pig was laid in the *umu* upon a bed
of steaming stones and covered over with layer upon
layer of fragrant leaves. Judd, meanwhile, had speared
half-a-dozen fish in the shallows. These he cleaned and
wrapped in neat packages of *ti* leaves. They were
placed around the pig, and a bunch of red bananas
laid on top of it all. Then more layers of leaves sealed

over the food and prevented the heat from escaping. Steam rose in tantalizing wisps and the dinner cooked slowly.

When at last the feast was ready, the steaming stones were pulled aside. There, smoking in its leafy wrappings, the pig lay golden and glowing, with rich juices running in little rivulets down its sides. A dish to tempt the palates of the gods; a feast to dream about on an empty stomach! The fish were cooked to a turn, and Terii set oysters to bake in shells of coconut cream.

The four companions squatted flat on the ground and fell upon the food with greedy fingers. Judd and Ken vied laughingly with one another in the manner of proper Polynesian eating: popping the food into their mouths with a loud sucking noise. The louder the noise the greater compliment to the food, in native belief. To eat silently being nothing short of rudeness.

"Only goes to show that manners are a matter of geography," scoffed Ken. "I always suspected it."

When the last bit of fish had been eaten and the final morsel of pork smacked over; when the mountainous platter of roasted bananas had disappeared and the coconut shells were licked clean, sleep seemed the order of the afternoon. Matu produced a roll of finely woven *hala* mats and spread them out in the cool shade of the palms.

"Here are mats for you, Americans," he smiled. "We have eaten much. There is sleep upon your eyelids. It is time to rest."

With sighs of deep content, Judd and Ken threw themselves down on the mats and relaxed in every nerve. The Samoans curled up in the sand and were instantly asleep. There was a breeze blowing across the coral shingle, bringing with it a weedy smell from the reef, not unpleasant, and a warm whiff of *frangipani*. The ocean shone with the furious glitter of late afternoon.

Ken sighed. "I ought to be looking for Polynesian ruins, but . . . there's always tomorrow!" His voice trailed off.

Judd stretched and yawned. "Oh, forget your blooming Polynesians for a while. What are ruins compared with this?"

Long ago the boy had learned the fine flavor which life might hold when Time is banished to limbo. How right and reasonable it then became to lie through the long hot hours on a mat of *hala*. . . . Growing up among Tahitians, Judd had come to share something of their recognition of time: not by the abstract of seconds, minutes, hours; but by the rhythm of the tides, the coming and going of the fish; by slumber and waking. Polynesians were spendthrifts of time, enjoying a legacy of inexhaustible hours.

As if Ken had read Judd's thoughts, he was saying drowsily: "How wise these natives are, really. We civilized men have been blinded by science. Have you ever read Ouspensky's *Tertium Organum?*"

"Lord—no!"

"You should. Ouspensky says there's no such thing as a past, and no future; only a sort of shifting, rhythmic present."

"Who cares. . . ." At that moment Judd was too content to ponder it out. In the cool shade of the palms, where fugitive shadows chased one another across the sand, the boy lay relaxed and reflective. California, the University—all the things his father had expected him to accomplish—these he would undertake when he was again free to order his own actions. But until such time—— "This is what I believe in," he thought. "It's the best there is to life."

He fell into a heavy, dreamless slumber.

The moon was full up when Judd was awakened by a booming sound of measured rhythm, like the beating of a supernatural drum: the surf's tireless charge upon the reef. The boy pulled himself up on one elbow and looked around. Ken was still lost in sleep—dreaming about Polynesian migrations, probably. Well, Judd thought, no more dreaming for him; not on a night like this. In the gloom he could make out the dark forms of the sleeping Samoans. The palms were motionless, their great fronds edged with moonlight, like splinters of crystal.

The boy arose and walked to the edge of the sea, looking out across the black waters to the distant reef. Somewhere off to the south a storm was brewing; big swells were moving down upon the atoll, long rollers of dark glass that curled their crests in lines of melted silver. The first breath of the land breeze stirred, cooled by its passage through the jungle; a ghost of a breeze; a shadow reft of its substance. The sky was spangled with unguessed millions of stars: other worlds, other suns.

How good a swim would seem! Judd stepped out of his worn ducks and took the water in a clean-curving dive. Moonlight glinted on his arched body. A soft enchantment seemed to catch him up in a magic free of earthly elements. What a pity that Ken couldn't swim. Nothing could be more fun than this!

He turned and swam out toward the black and distant reef, each movement of his arms dripping showers of liquid phosphorus. The roar of the surf increased its thunder; eddying currents plucked at him. Gulls, wheeling above the break, croaked hoarsely, like the ghosts of sailormen hauling round the phantom yards.

"Imagine the mainland, after this!" the boy said aloud. And as he spoke, the whole reef vibrated to a long roll of thunder and the air hummed: a hushed yet mighty sound that seemed to have its source not in the air above but in the very element beneath him.

In that ghostly hour of first dawn, when light and darkness mingled to make magic of all things, he swam leisurely back to shore.

Trade-wind clouds, darkly airy, were silhouetted against the dawn sky. The land breeze flowed gently seaward, stirring the broad blades of the banana trees. The morning was deeply still. Already hermit crabs were dragging their shell houses into the shade of the scrub. Gulls and ghost terns planed and wheeled above the smoking surf, light-of-gold shining on their wings. The immaculate beach stretched away and away, white and fair, and the boy's eye followed it to the place where its curve carried it beyond eye's reach; the sand looked as if it had been undisturbed since time's beginning.

Judd lighted a fire and fetched the sack of coffee that he had brought from the stores of the *Island*

*Queen.* Soon its pungent aroma reached the nostrils of the sleepers, and they stirred and stretched, as if called by some soundless voice.

"The smell of good coffee'll rouse the dead," the boy thought with a smile; and called: "*Haere mai!* Come and get it!"

The others sat up, sniffed at the fragrant aroma, then leaped to their feet and crowded around, each holding forth a coconut shell to be filled.

"We've still a whole free day ahead of us, Ken," Judd reminded his friend, as they squatted there in the sand, sipping their hot coffee. "Do you still want to look for ruins?"

"I've got to," the other assured him. "My New England conscience won't let me pass up such a chance. Can't we take the canoe and go over to the big *motu* on the other side of the lagoon?"

"*E pae!*" Judd assented. "Let's go!"

## CHAPTER XII   TIGER SHARK

TERII AND MATU elected to remain behind. Those
rock-pools in the reef tempted them with promise of *varo* and *tanurés* and sea-porcupines. Out came
their fish-spears, and their brown faces beamed with
happy smiles of anticipation.

"We'll be back by sundown," Judd promised, as he
shoved the canoe into the water.

Ken flung half-a-dozen green drinking-nuts into

the canoe and, wading out knee-deep, climbed aboard. Judd leaped into the stern and picked up the paddle. The canoe slid silently across the lagoon under the swift impulsion of his strokes. Although the sun was but a few degrees above the horizon, the customary freshness of morning was lacking. A grayish mist filmed the lower sky, and it occurred to Ken that these atolls, deprived of the sun, were unbelievably oppressive. He was sensible of a steadily mounting heat.

"Give me your knife, Judd, and I'll open some coconuts."

Judd fished in one pocket, then the other. "I've lost it—no, wait; here it is." He handed it over.

Ken hacked off the end of a nut with the sharp, eight-inch blade, and passed the coconut to Judd. Then he opened another nut for himself, tilted back his head to let the cool refreshing juice trickle down his throat. The juice of the green nut is slightly tangy, like carbonated water; cool even on warm days; more sustaining than food. It is very different from the thick, sweetish "milk" familiar to the civilized world.

Glancing back over his shoulder, Judd saw that dark masses of cloud were gathering in the southeast, mounting and widening as they spread toward the sun. But still there was no coolness in the overcast sky: the air was moist and hot and tense. With the vanishing sun, color bleached from lagoon and sky.

"It feels as if rain were on the way, Judd."

"Wind, more likely," the other answered. "But not for some hours. We'll be back before trouble blows up."

The thrust of Judd's paddle sent the slim canoe half a length nearer the distant *motu*. A school of *ahia* fled before them like arrowheads winged with silver; a turtle, disturbed by the swish of the paddle, sank silently, fathoms deep. Far across the lagoon a fish leaped suddenly into the air, pirouetting like a playful harlequin before it fell back with a resounding splash. The lagoon was teeming and alive. On bright days the fish sought out coral caverns in whose cool shadows they might hide; but when the skies were overcast they ventured forth in their everlasting search for food: preying and preyed upon in nature's harsh law of survival.

Sharks had been cruising around, but they were the harmless kind—gray with black-tipped dorsals. Now Judd descried another dorsal that brought him up in alarm: a triangle of polished steel. There was something sinister in the stealth of its motion. "A big one," the boy thought, and he knew a twinge of concern as the dorsal paused, then approached the canoe, warily. It circled around, submerged, disappeared. . . .

"Did you see the size of that shark!" Ken exclaimed.

And Judd found himself murmuring under his breath: "*Ma'o e! E matai tu!*"—more than half convinced of the efficacy of that old shark-chant. The words fell upon the charged air like stones dropping into a well.

Off to starboard the water darkened as the long, sinister form rose again toward the surface and the polished triangle once more cleft the water. Judd, from his elevation in the stern, could see that the shark was probably twice the length of the canoe: twenty-eight or thirty feet at least, he decided. Now it approached in leisurely fashion, closer and closer, until the boy could see its attendant escort of pilot fish, glittering like spoonbait in flashes of gold and blue. Ken, in the act of opening another coconut, paused, knife in hand, to give a low whistle of alarm.

"Say, Judd——"

But Judd had halted the canoe and was splashing with his paddle. Swerving sharply to one side the shark darted by, rolling slightly in passing. Its belly gleamed white, and now along its sides Judd could see the mottled markings which proclaimed its species: tiger shark. He breathed more freely when it had passed astern and he commenced to paddle once more, sending the canoe ahead with forceful strokes. He'd be glad when they reached the *motu*.

"I didn't like the looks of that fellow," he confessed. "I'm glad he's gone."

But a second later Ken shouted in consternation: "Look! He's on the other side of us!"

As Judd turned he saw the great snout, with jaws agape, almost directly beneath him. He raised the paddle and smashed it down upon the shark's nose—its one tender spot. The fish whipped its length in flight. But as it turned, the thrash of its powerful tail lifted the stern of the canoe high out of the water. The two boys were hurled headlong into the air. Judd knew a flash of panic: Ken, who couldn't swim—— Then the outrigger struck him a stunning blow across the head. His senses reeled. He tried to cry out, to fight his way to the surface. But down, down he sank into illimitable depths of blue. . . .

When his mind cleared—after how many seconds he never knew—he found himself still in the water, clinging to the outrigger. The canoe had righted itself in falling. There was a mist before the boy's eyes; a fog in his brain. He remembered then. . . . Ken, where was he? Judd tried to shout. No sound issued from his throat. Ken, who couldn't—— He saw his friend then. Ken, treading water, had placed himself between Judd and the shark; the knife glittered in his hand. He set up a desperate splashing. The steel-blue dorsal, a periscope of death, was closing in, in ever-decreasing circles.

Even as Judd felt power returning to his body, the shark seemed to pause: a split second of respite. Ken had stopped splashing, every nerve taut. Judd struck out for his friend's side.

With light's own speed the shark charged. There was a stunning impact—the flash of a knife. Water lashed to foam. A cry of anguish. . . . A sandpaper hide raked Judd's arm from elbow to shoulder. With his face flat to the water, the boy saw the great fish turn over far below the surface. Blood was flowing from the wound in its belly. Spots of red widened in the foam.

"Ken! *Ken!* Are you all right?"

Ken's face, white as paper. . . . As Judd reached

his side he threw an arm around him; he saw a line, clean as a knife-cut, ripped across his friend's shoulder. He helped Ken into the canoe, his breath coming in gasps. With vast relief Judd saw that it was only a flesh wound, bleeding profusely but not deep. He ripped the shirt from his back, tore it into strips and bound up the wound. Ken, who couldn't swim, who was afraid of the water. . . . Ken, the bookworm, had saved his life.

"Man alive! What a shark-fighter you turned out to be!" And Judd's voice was husky.

Ken struggled to grin and tried to sit up. "Guess— I'll have something to tell . . . the Museum. . . ." He dropped over on the floor of the canoe in a dead faint.

Judd pulled up to a curve of sandy beach and the prow of the canoe grated dully on the shingle. Palm trees trooped almost to the water's edge, their glistening fronds motionless in the still air. A flock of water birds rose with startled cries, sounding an alarm that seemed unnaturally loud in this silent place. Judd helped his friend into the shade of a wide-branching *pukatea* tree, then went in search of some limes to cauterize the wound in Ken's shoulder. Half an hour later the operation was complete. The shoulder was bound up in a ragged but professional-looking bandage made from Judd's only shirt. Both boys were shivering in their wet clothes. The wind, freshening from the ocean, seemed cold as it struck their chilled bodies.

"I'm going to build a fire," Judd said, "and then I'll see if I can find a couple of breadfruit. Warm food is what we need." He reached into his pocket and pulled forth a pulpy mass of wet matches. "Well! Guess this is my cue to make fire with wood!"

"That's a terrible job," Ken protested. "Let's be content with some coconuts——"

"No. I'm frozen and so are you. Wait till I find a firestick." He searched about in the undergrowth until he found a piece of wood that was hard and bone-dry; it was about as large as his forearm. He shaved off a sliver of the end, whittled it to a sharp point, then he propped the larger piece against a rock. Seating himself on a stone, he gripped the pointed stick with both hands, moved it rapidly back and forth upon the surface of the larger wood until gradually a groove began to appear.

Now the boy's hands were racing back and forth, back and forth. A tinder of wood-dust began to form at the lower end of the groove. Faster, still faster his hands worked. Sweat broke out on his forehead and ran down into his eyes. His breath came rapidly. A wisp of smoke rose from the dust. Leaning forward swiftly to cup the precious smoke with both hands, Judd blew gently upon the little pile of wood-dust. The dust began to glow. Very gingerly he laid on some bits of dry twigs and leaves. A flame burst forth and the fire was going.

"Phew! It's no wonder the old natives never let their fires go out," Ken exclaimed.

"And no wonder the young ones buy matches!" Judd disappeared into the jungle. When he returned, Ken saw that the other had found two breadfruit, several bananas, and two large blue crabs whose claws were tied with a twist of bark. The fire died to a bed of fine embers and now Judd set about preparing their lunch. Into the hot embers he dropped the crabs, covering them with leaves so they would steam through. Then he placed the breadfruit and bananas in the coals where they would remain until their charred black skin would pop open. Then he slashed open the end of two drinking-nuts and set them to rest carefully against a rock.

"*Haeré mai tamaa!* Come and get it!" Judd was busily peeling off the charred rinds of the breadfruit, breaking them into smoking halves so that the flaky white meat would have a chance to cool. Then he lifted the *ti* leaves away from the crabs and Ken saw that they had changed from blue to red. The bananas were charred and popping with juice; Judd skinned them gingerly and laid them on a leaf.

"I thought that feast yesterday was the tops," Ken mumbled over a mouthful of breadfruit. "But——"

For the next few moments the only sound was that of their munching.

"You've got two hands to my one," Ken complained.

"I'm lucky to have any hands at all," his friend returned. "I suppose you know you saved my life——"

"Oh, rats! I reckon you saved mine; if you hadn't given me that knife to open coconuts . . ."

"And I thought I'd lost it!"

"Where did you ever learn to put on a bandage like this?"

"You have to learn such things where there aren't any doctors around," Judd assured him. "Gee, Ken! Matu himself couldn't have made a better job of knifing that shark than you did!" His face was alight with admiration.

Ken beamed happily. "Swimming's easy," was all

he said. He was deeply moved by his friend's praise, but embarrassed by it at the same time. To turn the conversation, he lifted his coconut shell and drank deeply. "Coconuts—what would these islands have been without 'em?"

"They wouldn't have been inhabited, that's certain. I don't believe there's another tree in the world that's so useful. It's food and drink for the natives. The leaves make his roof; the trunk, the frame of his house. . . ."

"That's only part of it," the other added. "The fiber around the nut is used for everything from fishline to tying rafters and beams together. The ancient Polynesians used to weave it into clothes."

"And the ripe meat's grand fish bait," Judd assured him, "and food for dogs, pigs, chickens, and humans. As for the roots—the old people brew a medicine out of 'em for fevers!"

"You haven't forgotten copra?" Ken suggested. "That's as important as anything else. It's the only native industry."

"That's right! Without it they'd never have a *centime* to buy anything, and it furnishes half the soap, cold cream, margarine, and candles for the civilized world. Who ever heard of another tree that produces food, clothing, and shelter—and is an industry into the bargain?"

"But say, this isn't discovering any ruins!" cried Ken. "Let's go."

"Don't you think you'd better take it easy?" Judd suggested. "That's no mean bite you got. . . . We could camp here tonight and go back to join Matu and Terii in the morning."

"What are you trying to do—make a sissy out of me? Let's get going!"

Off they went across the *motu*, poking here and there in the dense scrub. But if the ancient Polynesians had ever passed this way in their transpacific migrations they had left no record of it.

"We haven't found a darned thing since we've been here," Ken grumbled.

"Except enough black-lip to make us rich—if we can ever come back for it," Judd threw in. "Don't be an ingrate!"

"You know what I mean," the other answered. "The old Polynesians followed the eastward sea currents from Asia; they came this way in their canoes long before Columbus discovered America. And at most of these islands they stopped: either wrecked, or putting in for fresh food and water. They buried the ones that died in just such islands as this, and built temples to their gods. It's by such things that we scientists have pieced together, bit by bit, the story of their migrations."

"Well," said Judd, matter-of-factly, "if they didn't stop here they didn't, and that's all there is to it."

But Ken's disappointment increased with every foot they traveled. "They *must* have stopped here. How about those wild chickens we saw? You don't think those chickens *flew* here from Asia, do you?"

"They might have been put ashore by the skipper of the *St. Etienne*," Judd suggested. "Or even, as far as that goes, by the men of the *Antipodes!*"

"Lord!" groaned Ken. "I never thought of that."

"What would you scientists do if it weren't for a few practical minds!"

The wind was variable, blowing now from one quarter, now from another; a heavy surf was breaking over the outer reef. The boys watched the seas gathering far out, rising in sheer walls that seemed higher than the island itself, charging upon the shore to burst into a smoke of high-flung mist and spray. It was an awe-inspiring sight and not without a certain fascination. Between the breaking of one sea and the gathering of the next, the water poured back over the walls of black reef, leaving fish floundering in the hollows. Out along the horizon the sky was a brassy gray, while higher up dark clouds were racing before a wind which was still too high to make itself felt below. Out beyond the breakers a heavy calm flattened the ocean to greasy opaqueness.

"Looks like a bad squall," Ken said. "Perhaps we'd better try to get back to Matu and Terii and forget about ruins."

"I've a hunch it may be more than a squall," Judd returned. He was too experienced an islander to disregard the rapidly increasing danger signals. "We'd better look for some kind of shelter. How's the shoulder?"

"Okay! Let's go."

The air had become oppressively hot. Sweat streamed from every pore in their bodies. They reached the shelter of a group of coral rocks that had been piled up in some previous cataclysm and sank down within its protective lee.

"Golly—the sky's getting black!"

"And look at that water!" Judd cast an anxious glance about, speculating as to which direction the wind would set in. If it should be from the southeast, at this season of the year it could mean but one thing. . . .

Ken was saying, "You don't think we're in for a hurricane?"

His friend shook his head, wishing that he could

convince himself. The coppery light had vanished and the sky thickened like a somber northern twilight. The wind was rising now, and it seemed to be settling in from one direction: southeast. . . . They could see it before they felt it; darkening the surface of the water as it passed; whipping up angry whitecaps in its relentless advance. The first breath of it, tonic wth life, fanned their hot faces.

"Well—not much to that," was Ken's comment.

But Judd was busy reinforcing their shelter with coral blocks and stones. There came a second wind, a fierce gust this time, accompanied by an ominous boom as gathering seas struck at the barrier reef. Slowly the ocean was becoming a procession of advancing mountains, awe-inspiring and terrible. They marched down upon the atoll in long gray lines and the island began to quiver beneath their onslaught. To Ken there was something profoundly disturbing in the sensation of insecurity beneath them, the realization that this small atoll, anchored to the ocean floor only by tiny coral polyps, was shaking in the grip of elemental forces. Vana Vana was scarcely fifteen feet above sea level at its highest point, and there was nothing to break the force of the seas between here and Asia.

Judd was explaining, "In this part of the Pacific

hurricanes travel in a wide curve. Perhaps it'll circle around." He didn't know a great deal about these tropical revolving storms, except that they originated in the doldrum belts on either side of the equator, revolving counterclockwise above the line, and clockwise below it, due to the trades blowing in from northeast and southeast.

The boys could hear the dull thud of falling coconuts on every hand. The palms were beginning to writhe like whiplashes, and the air was filled with flying fronds, seemingly so delicate, yet any one of which could have killed them with a blow. A scudding film, shot through with strange lights, was drawing over the surface of the sea.

Seeing it, Judd said, "Here she comes, Ken."

The slate-gray film, extending the length of the visible horizon, was moving in out of the southeast. Sea and sky were fused in the one color. At first it was only a whispering drone of sound: gradually it deepened in volume to a roar. The rain leaped upon them.

During the moments that followed, all nature seemed to have gone mad. The scream of the wind was cut through by a whining hum—like the noise of worlds humming through interstellar space. The sea flattened beneath the wind, boiling with fury. It was impossible to face the wind and breathe. The boys crouched behind their rude shelter, flat on the ground. The very island was vibrating beneath their bodies, filling their souls with awe.

An unceasing deluge stung them with fury, set them shaking in their thin clothes. The wind doubled on itself and increased its force. Breadfruit trees were being uprooted and swept across the lagoon. Palms, stripped of leaves, bent over to the ground and remained in that position, without thrashing, but trembling as with a mighty ague. The air was filled with flying branches, boulders of coral, clouds of sand. Coconuts hurtled past the two crouching figures with the force of projectiles. The rain struck in horizontal sheets, seeming to leap from crest to crest of the waves.

Minutes lengthened into hours. Time was wiped out. All the accustomed signs by which men note the passage of the hours had been obliterated. Only a fury of sound was left to a world spinning through space.

As the tide turned, the waves increased in size. Wind and moon were joining forces to pile the Pacific Ocean on the shores of this tiny atoll. Thousands of leagues of sea hurled forward on the breath of the hurricane. . . . Judd tried to speak some word of reassurance, but the wind shoved his voice down his throat.

As the hurricane mounted, the weight of rain eased. But now the sea was rising. Slowly, surely—brought about by the sharp drop in atmospheric pressure. With each fresh onslaught the water reached farther up the shingle, its hungry fingers seeking the two who cowered behind their shelter. Soon it was imperative that they abandon their barricade and seek another farther inland. The next wave might reach them, its back-wash drag them with it into the sea. They began to crawl, flat on their stomachs, back into the under-growth where the elevation was slightly higher. They were in constant danger from flying branches and rocks. They crawled into the lee of a large boulder that was half covered with a tangle of scrub. With his knife Judd tried to hack away some of the branches to make more room for their bodies. The ground was running with water—rain and sea—and spongy; it gave beneath their weight. Soon they had space enough to lie at full length. They gathered all the rocks within arm's reach to form a rude barricade. Sea, rain, hail beat at them, stung them, pounded them into the ground. They buried their faces in their arms, too frightened to more than breathe; too exhausted to pray. It was the end of a world.

Every sense became dulled, weary of tumult. Their ears no longer could distinguish one sound from another. Only an overwhelming assault of thunder, reverberating through their souls like the trumpets of doom: the sound of worlds colliding, splintering into space, spiraling to oblivion in the darkness that lay beyond the stars. All sense of danger vanished. Annihilation was momentary, destruction inevitable. They were no longer human beings in a world of men; they were motes whirling into chaos. What was their strength of body or of spirit against these powers of darkness?

They had no sense of time's passage. So imperceptible was the storm's easing that at first they did not notice it. But the wind was beginning slowly to diminish; the intermittent pauses between gusts were each time of greater duration. The swinging seas still crashed the outer reef in cataracts of thunder; spray sprang at the low-hanging sky. Judd lifted his head cautiously above the barricade. The wind struck at him, but now it held less of menace.

He looked about him warily. "Anyway, we won't starve," he shouted, close to his friend's ear. "Coconuts—crabs—fish. The beach covered with 'em."

They set about making their shelter as secure as possible, for it would be hours before they could attempt to reach the lagoon. Judd searched for another firestick, and once more set about laboriously kindling a fire with wood alone. It seemed as if he would never succeed. But at long last there came a wisp of smoke, a glow. He sheltered it with his body while Ken aided with a cupped hand. Smoke rose from the tinder and the boys placed slivers of wood upon the growing flame. The searching wind fanned it to a blaze. They piled on more wood; it steamed, smoked, but burned in spite of itself. Close to its circle of warmth they huddled to dry their wet rags, shivering with cold, their teeth chattering in their heads.

The rain had eased its fury while the wind droned above their heads in a whining wail. The fire blazed forth bravely. Smoke and sparks, lifting above the coral barrier, were swept away into the outer darkness. Judd rose to his knees and crept cautiously a short way off, gathering such food as he could find. He brought back a couple of fish, cast up by the sea, and these he threw into the fire to roast. Then he discovered a cracked coconut, close at hand; its meat was brackish with sea water, but it eased the ache in their throats.

At length Judd pulled the fish from the embers; and when the two friends had eaten, they sank back once more within the fire's warm circle while the storm swung in its wide curve to the northeast, off into the empty spaces of the world beyond.

Judd didn't speak of the fear that had haunted his mind since the beginning of the storm: the *Island Queen*—suppose she had been torn from her anchorage and piled up on the reef! She was anchored in the lee of the *motu*. But so low was the land that it was a doubtful protection. Judd knew that if the brig were wrecked, he and Ken would be castaway on an unknown atoll with three rogues and a pack of headhunters. He forced the prospect from his mind.

"Say, Judd!" Ken exclaimed, sitting up suddenly as a thought struck him. "I just remembered. Did you think the pearls weren't safe enough under the floor board in our cabin?"

"Why—what do you mean?" Judd knew a sinking feeling at his stomach's pit.

"I meant to speak about it yesterday," Ken went on, "but I forgot. . . . Just before we pushed off from the brig, while you were waiting in the canoe and I was down in our cabin, I happened to think of the pearls. I don't know why, but I lifted the board— just to be sure they were all right. They were gone, and I thought that you——"

"Gone!" Judd's voice sounded strangled.

"Yes," Ken returned. "I thought you'd moved them to some safer place. Great Scott! They haven't——"

The two boys looked at each other with sick eyes. "Bergstrom must have found out," Ken whispered. Judd nodded dumbly, unable to speak.

"Lord!" Ken groaned. "If I'd only remembered to speak about it before we left!"

"What good would that have done? The fat's in the fire now. The pearls weren't worth much, except for those two Matu found. But Bergstrom will know by those that we've found black-lip shell."

"What do you suppose he'll do?"

Judd shrugged. "Lord knows! There's nothing for us to do but brazen it out." He leaped to his feet. "I hope we can locate the canoe. If not, we'll have to go on foot and wade the shallows. That'll take hours. We'd better get going."

They crawled out of their shelter, stood upright painfully, and stretched their aching bones. A scene of desolation met their eyes. Hardly a coconut palm was left standing. The few that had escaped the fury of the wind had been stripped of leaves. They were as ugly as broom handles, incredibly transformed when shorn of their graceful plumage. Boulders of coral, torn off by the violence of the sea, were piled along shore. The boys picked their way toward the lagoon through a maze of uprooted trees.

On the inner beach the destruction had not been

so great. Quantities of dead fish lay on the sand where they had been stranded by the receding water.

"Well, this is where we left the canoe, but—where is it?" Judd tried to keep the note of anxiety from his voice.

There was no sign of the canoe.

"If it was carried out into the lagoon that's the last of it," Ken muttered.

"Yes—but it may have been blown down the beach and filled up with sand. Let's look for it."

And it turned out that that was what had happened: the canoe had been blown down the inner beach, its outrigger ripped off; now it lay half on its side, wedged in between two boulders. A score of crabs that had taken refuge out of the storm scurried away as Judd emptied the canoe of sand. The boy fastened a new *purao* pole in place of the old outrigger, and was just about to drag it into the lagoon when Ken's startled voice brought him up with a jump.

"*Judd!* Look here! What's that?"

Judd turned back. He saw that Ken was peering excitedly into a thick clump of scrub that was filled with palm fronds and the aftermath of the storm. At first he could distinguish nothing. But as he approached his friend he felt his pulse leap. For what he saw—— Ken had parted the thicket and was peering at what appeared to be the doorway of a half-subterranean building, or room; looking more like a large sarcophagus than anything else Judd could think of. It was a sort of natural cave in the earth, built up for a foot or two above ground and roofed over with slabs of coral which had long since become encased with convolvulus and clambering vines. Judd saw a slab of coral standing on edge before the entrance of the cave.

"Lord!" Ken breathed. "What a find!"

Judd knew that he was looking at the half-obliterated work of men long since vanished. And he felt as he had often felt in Tahiti when stumbling upon some ancient burial cave in the mountains: a sense of the remote antiquity of the race which had crossed the Pacific in the childhood of the world.

"It is *tabu!*" he cried sharply, instinctively. It was his first reaction. And then he thought, "How foolish: that's native talk."

But Ken was already pulling at the heavy coral slab. It took the two of them to move it. The coral was as white as bone and gave off a hollow, drumlike sound when they struck it. Then on hands and knees the two boys crawled into the cave. The floor was of white sand, as smooth and untroubled and white as a bowl of sugar. As their eyes became accustomed to the gloom they peered about eagerly. Across one end of the cave was a shelf hewn out of coral—the very foundation of the island itself; and upon this shelf a row of skulls grinned back at these intruders. Judd had to remind himself once again that this *tabu* stuff was nonsense. But just the same there was something disturbing in that row of grinning skulls, and the boy knew that he was looking upon a sight that had never been seen by the eyes of man since those Polynesian warriors, in dim history, had placed the skulls in position and walled up this burial cave.

"Judd, look at those weapons!" Ken's voice was trembling with excitement; he could scarcely contain himself. The discovery of pearls or of gold was as nothing compared to this. This—why, this was what ethnologists dreamed about!

Judd saw a variety of weapons laid out in orderly range: spears and clubs of ironwood, dark with age. Ken's eager hands were examining them. "I've never seen wood like it," he muttered. "Feel it. It's like iron."

"That's what it's called—ironwood," Judd assured him. "*Aito*, the Tahitians call it. But there's no ironwood on Vana Vana. They must have brought those weapons here from some other place."

"Look at the shaft of this spear! This is *casuarina*

wood. I'm sure of that. They brought it from Malay, or India."

Judd watched his friend with vast delight, in spite of himself caught up in the excitement of the other's enthusiasm. This meant more, really, than pearls or black-lip or gold. . . .

"And look at those bowls. Oh, boy!"

On the floor stood two elongated bowls of dark polished greenstone, such as the Maoris of New Zealand carved with such skill and beauty. Judd knew that he was in the presence of a genuinely important scientific discovery. His heart beat high.

"Ken," he whispered. "Look—over there."

On a sort of wooden couch lay a form long and shapeless but suggestively human. What might once have been the head was large and round, wrapped in layers of *tapa*, grotesque as a jack-o'-lantern. Bindings of coconut sennit wrapped the figure round in patterns of intricate beauty. By its side, where the hand might have been, was a war-club dark with age and of surpassing beauty in design. Ken picked it up reverently.

"Feel the weight of it, Judd. Look at this beautiful design." His voice quivered with the emotion of the discoverer.

The war-club was as black and nearly as heavy as

iron. The edges of its elliptical head were razor-sharp, while the handle had been designed for a grip of more than ordinary size. Mighty men, those early Polynesians. Judd felt it gingerly and marveled at the beautiful balance of such a ponderous weapon.

"Those old boys must have been as strong as lions," he said. "Imagine carrying this around with you in battle. . . ." He was caught up in the thrilling excitement of this discovery. Bergstrom, Malloy, the *Island Queen*—all vanished from his consciousness. Standing there in that dim cave, gazing upon the work of men dead these countless centuries, he knew to the full Ken's own enthusiasm. He understood, at last, what it might be that lured men to the end of the world in some imagined quest, and held them like prisoners in its potent spell. He dropped to his knees, examining a pictograph cut into a coral boulder. "Look, this is a turtle! And this bird—it might be an albatross. And this—what do you make of this, Ken?"

Ken knelt beside his friend, and together they tried to decipher the message graven into stone when the world was young. Ken shook his head sadly. "I give up. . . . We could spend weeks here, Judd, if only we had the time."

The other nodded, his eyes clouded with thought. "We *will* spend weeks here, Ken, one of these days.

We're coming back here, you and I—some day when we've put Axel Bergstrom where he belongs. There may be other burial caves on some of the other *motus*. Gee, Ken! This may be one of the scientific finds of the century!"

The other agreed warmly. "You never know. That's what gets you; anything is possible."

They stood there silent for a moment, touched with a sense of awe. Then reluctantly Judd returned to a world of reality. "We ought to be getting back to the ship," he grudged.

"Yes, I know, but——"

"I hate to leave, myself, Ken. But we'll come back—from Singapore, or from the ends of the world. We've got to come back!"

And so they emerged into the blinding sunlight, and replaced the coral slab over the entrance, then turned their backs unwillingly upon the cave and made their way to the canoe.

Half an hour later they reached the spot where they had left Matu and Terii the day before. But they found no sign of the two Samoans.

"You don't think anything could have happened to them in the storm, do you?" Ken asked anxiously.

"Of course not. They cut their teeth on hurricanes. They probably started back to the brig on foot, swimming the shallows and crossing the *motus* wherever they could. It'll take them hours to get there, but they'll manage it all right."

Judd ran up the sail and the outrigger fled across the lagoon, retracing its course to the *Island Queen*. So Bergstrom had found the two black pearls and the "seeds." . . . He knew about the shell. . . . Now what would the man do?

Things had stopped drifting. Was there a showdown ahead? Judd's smile was grim and his fingers tensed on the grip of the tiller.

## CHAPTER XIII  SHOW-DOWN

JUDD SCANNED the shore line of the distant *motu* in whose lee the *Island Queen* lay anchored. He was filled with anxiety. Was the brig there still, or had she piled up and gone to the locker of Davy Jones? No sign of her tophamper showed above the circlet of low land and his anxiety mounted. The upper rigging

could have carried away without serious damage
to the rest of the ship, but anchored as the brig was
among heavy coral patches, she would have been
utterly destroyed if she lay within the direct path of
the hurricane.

"You don't think the brig could have cracked up,
do you?" Ken was asking anxiously.

"She's safe as a church," Judd assured him, and
wished that he could believe it himself.

Then, rounding the tip of the *motu*, they saw with
intense relief that the brig still swung to her anchor.
Judd wanted to shout for joy. Ken let out a yell of
relief, for he had not been deceived by his companion's glib answer. The brig's two topmasts had
carried away; rigging hung loose and idly dangling in
the wind. She had dragged her anchor but still she
held clear of the reef. Grand little ship! The boys'
hearts gave a surge of pride; that little ship was their
only connection with the outside world of men and
events; she was their only hope of escape from the coil
of circumstance which had imprisoned them. The
thought of her destruction was a possibility which
neither of them cared to face.

"She looks pretty well banged up," Ken said
dubiously, as they drew closer.

"Not as bad as she looks. It won't take the Samoans

long to get her shipshape again. Gosh, we're lucky,
Ken. We might have been marooned here for the rest
of our lives with those——"

"I know. I've been thinking about that, too."

"Have you formed any sort of plan, Judd, for
getting control of things?"

The other nodded. "Yes, but the whole thing hinges
on getting the key to the firearms locker. Bergstrom
carries it in his pocket all the time. Without guns we
couldn't do a thing. But with them we could get the
drop on Bergstrom and Malloy, cow the Solomon
Islanders, and sail for New Zealand."

Ken sighed. "Sounds easy, the way you say it.
But——"

The outrigger sailed up under the brig's counter
and the two boys clambered aboard. Axel Bergstrom,
seated in a deck chair, looked up from a sheaf of charts
which he was examining. He was in his shirt sleeves,
his linen coat hanging over the back of his chair.
Whatever dark thought may have been in the man's
mind, his smile was smooth and bland, his manner
affable. Judd marveled at the man's gift for dissem-
bling, and the thought struck him suddenly that the
pearls might not have been discovered by Bergstrom
after all. Perhaps Malloy found them, or even one of
the Solomon Islanders. . . . The boy looked about

for the Australian, but Malloy was nowhere in sight.

"Well, where have you two been?" Bergstrom's tone was noncommittal.

"The storm caught us on the western *motu*," Judd answered him. "We couldn't get back till it blew itself out. Much damage done?" He looked aloft, hoping to forestall further questioning.

"Enough—the men are already at work repairing. Where are Matu and Terii?"

"Aren't they back yet?"

The Swede shook his head. "No—devil take them! And neither are those blasted blacks. I suppose they're cowering away somewhere till the sun comes out. We're clearing for Singapore just as soon as you and the men get this ship in condition. If you need me I'll be below."

The two boys looked blankly after him.

"Don't you suppose he found the pearls, Judd?"

"If he did you'd never know it."

"Well, somebody did all right! If not Bergstrom then it was Malloy. Maybe they plan to go up to Singapore, turn the specie into cash, and return here to prospect the lagoon."

"Maybe. . . ." Judd shook a puzzled head. "We'll know soon enough."

Siva, Falé, and Taupo were in the upper rigging, fishing new spars in place of the ones that had been damaged by the storm. Judd joined them, and together they spent the long hours of the afternoon patching, tightening, painting, getting gear aloft shipshape once again. As afternoon waned and the sun dropped lower, Judd found himself concerned for Matu and Terii. They should be returning by now, even though they must come on foot around the whole weary circlet of the *motus*. As for the Solomon Islanders, it was evident that they were making the most of their shore leave. No telling when they would get back.

As the boy worked there aloft, testing the footropes that hung in their stirrups beneath the t'gallant yard, his eye was attracted by a flutter of paper on the deck below. The wind was rattling the sheaf of charts which Bergstrom had left behind him. Then the boy's pulse leaped and his heart began to hammer—he noticed that the Swede's white linen jacket was still hanging where its owner had left it over the back of the deck chair. There was just a chance . . . He beckoned urgently to Falé. Swiftly and silently the two slid down the shrouds and crossed over to the deck chair. While Falé kept a wary eye cocked toward the companionway, Judd ran his hands quickly through the pockets—first one, then the other. A jingle of metal sang in his ears. Triumph swelled in his throat.

"We've got 'em!" he whispered exultantly, hardly able to contain himself. "Take these keys, Falé, go below, and try to unlock the firearms locker. Don't open the door—just leave it unlocked. And remember, if you make a sound——"

The Samoan fled on silent feet toward the companionway.

"It *must* be one of those keys!" the boy assured himself fervently. "It's *got* to be!" He stood there taut with eagerness, waiting, not daring to hope, scarcely daring to breathe. It seemed in this moment as if everything in the world, his world, hung in the balance.

Shortly Falé reappeared, his dark face glowing with achievement. And Judd had hardly returned the keys to the Swede's pocket when Bergstrom's step sounded on the stair. The two boys turned hastily away and pretended to busy themselves coiling down rope; and it seemed to Judd that the man must surely hear the pounding of his heart. But Bergstrom, unsuspicious, picked up his charts, removed his coat from the back of the deck chair, and disappeared once more below.

Then shortly through the open skylight of the main cabin came the clink of the decanter.

"What luck, Falé?" Judd questioned eagerly.

"*Ai!*" the native whispered back excitedly. "It was the little round key. . . . The door groaned when I opened it, but Malloy was snoring in his cabin like a thunder god. No one heard."

"And the firearms?"

"*Aué!* But there are enough for an army!"

"You left the door of the locker ajar?"

"*E pai*, yes!"

The firearms locker was at the foot of the companionway steps. The door to Malloy's cabin lay just beyond it. Bergstrom's cabin was at the farther end of the narrow passage. Events were playing into the boy's hands. If only Malloy's Solomon Islanders didn't return before morning! If only something would happen to bring Malloy and Bergstrom together in the main cabin. . . .

Ken popped up from below. "Say, you look as if you'd come into an inheritance!" he cried. "What the——"

His friend silenced him with a swift hand over his lips, drew him aside, and explained the plan. Ken listened, and his breathing quickened, and his eyes grew rounder with excitement.

"Golly!" he breathed. "Do you suppose we can pull it off?"

The sun went down in a blaze of fire. Dusk rose up from the sea, investing the little ship with palpitant mystery. The boys lighted the riding-lights and the lantern that hung from the mainmast. They were all tense with expectancy. Now that events were reaching a climax it seemed beyond human endurance to have to wait, quietly, for something to happen.

Then somewhere below a door slammed.

"What door's that?" Ken whispered. "I'm jumpy as a cat."

"The door to Malloy's cabin," Taupo offered. "He'll be up here in a second. Watch out. . . ."

But presently they heard Malloy's cockney tones issuing up through the skylight of Bergstrom's cabin. A glow of yellow sprang into being from the room below as the lamp was lighted.

"They're together—what luck!" Judd could

scarcely credit their good fortune. He wanted to shout, to jump, to yell.

"At last," Ken breathed, "we're getting the breaks."

The three Samoans emerged from the shadows and moved toward Judd, awaiting the order that would send them into action. On silent feet Judd and Ken crossed over and peered down through the open sky-light. Their eyes widened at what they saw: Malloy sat out of range of their vision, but Bergstrom was almost beneath them, his back turned toward them. The light from the lantern made a circle of gold on the green-topped table. The boys strained forward. They saw two small boxes lying on top of the table. Judd's breath caught when he saw the contents of those boxes. A little thrill ran along his nerves.

Two black pearls, spaced from each other by tufts of cotton. Under the glow of the hanging lantern they seemed almost to breathe and have being. Judd hadn't realized that they were so lovely. A little pile of "seeds" held a slumbering warmth like the tawny flush of first dawn. And those pearls were Judd's own! His and Ken's and Matu's and Terii's. They had risked their lives for them. They had fought the shark and the *feké*, and now——

Bergstrom let the pearls slip lingeringly through his fingers. He smiled oddly. "Beautiful, beautiful," he murmured, more to himself than to his companion. "Look at these two blacks! Blacks used to be worthless until an empress of France wore them around her throat and made a fashion of them. Black-lip breeds black pearls. There must be more where these came from. . . ."

The two black pearls lay there in that white palm like the dark, unwinking eyes of an idol.

Malloy chuckled quietly. "Quite a 'aul, I will say. The pearls ain't worth much, Axel, but that black-lip —— And those pin-feathered kids thinkin' they could put a deal like that over on us!"

"Tor Jansen seemed to think he'd seen large patches of shell near the wreck, but I thought we'd clean up the gold first. . . ." His voice trailed off to a thread of sound. The little sea-stones, cupped in the palm of his hand, appeared to have cast a spell over him. His voice was soft as he said, "I once knew a man, a scientist, who claimed that the most beautiful pearl was only the tomb of a worm. The Chinese knew better: they called pearls Tears of Celestial Beings. Poets, those Chinese. . . ."

Judd motioned swiftly to the Samoans. "*Now!*" he breathed. "You, Ken, stay on deck and sound a warning if the blacks put in an appearance."

Four shadowy figures padded across the deck, silent

as cats, their bare feet making no whisper of sound. They stole down the stairs, scarcely daring to breathe. At the foot of the steps they paused, listening with every nerve. Bergstrom's door, at the corridor's end, was closed. The door to the firearms locker was just as Falé had left it. It swung silently to Judd's touch. Siva held the lantern aloft as Judd armed each of the natives and slipped cartridges into the chamber of a .45 for himself. They crept down the corridor, noiseless as shadows. The low murmur of the two men's voices issued through the heavy oak paneling.

With a pulse hammering in his throat, Judd grasped the doorknob of Bergstrom's cabin. He turned it. The door swung under his hand, squeaking loudly on rusty hinges. The men at the table whipped about.

"Up with your hands!" Judd threw out. "Make it fast!"

"Damn you——" Bergstrom reached for his hip.

Judd's trigger finger pulled. The porthole behind the Swede's head splintered with a crash. The man's hands went up.

"I mean business, Bergstrom! The next shot won't be for the porthole. Siva, tie them up. Falé, keep Malloy covered."

The scar on Malloy's cheek bone was a line of purple. Amazement stamped his features. He could not credit his senses. Bergstrom's face was a mask of white in which his eyes were like the unsheathing of twin blue blades. "You fools—you can't get away with this!"

Judd laughed. "Watch us!"

With stout sharkline the natives were binding the men's hands behind them. Then their feet. Judd was at the table scooping the pearls into the boxes. He glanced at the cases of specie piled against the wall and said, "It *was* a pretty good 'aul, Malloy. Pearls and gold. . . . And maybe the Colonial Government offers a reward for you two! Anyway—we're going to find out."

Bergstrom's reply was a strangled curse. Malloy appeared stupefied by the turn of events. The Samoans threw the two bound men to the floor. Judd stood over them, looking down. "Now listen, you two!" he rapped. "Your game's up. We're sailing for New Zealand. You'll get what's coming to you and it'll be plenty."

"You've got nothing on us," Bergstrom ground out.

"How about Karl Kassel?" the boy suggested.

"He died of black-water, and you can't prove he didn't!" The Swede's eyes were like ice on fire.

"Tor Jansen shot him," Judd returned. "And you

dumped him overboard. Accomplice to murder, I believe they call it. I heard you tell Malloy, and Matu saw the whole thing and will testify to it."

The man's only answer was a sound of inchoate rage. Leaving the men bound and helpless in the main cabin, the boys hurried aloft. As they emerged from the companionway they heard happy shouts that issued almost it seemed out of the sea itself. A second later Matu and Terii were scrambling up the chains, to stand dripping on the deck.

"*Aué!*" cried Matu. "What a swim we have had."

"Swim?"

"*Ai!* The eaters-of-men are building their fires on the *motu* to the east. We were afraid they would kill and cook us. We have swum many miles."

The midnight tide was setting on the shoulder of a southwest wind. "There's a breeze lifting," Judd cried. "What do you say, Ken?"

"I say up-anchor, Cap'n!" the other came back at him. "But what about the Solomon Islanders?"

"The Colonial Government can pick 'em up when they get back here with His Britannic Majesty's flag."

"Ho! Time and tide wait for no man!"

Measuring the breeze against his cheek Judd called the order: "Heave short! Get off the gaskets. Stand by with the lifeboat to tow if necessary."

To the accompaniment of a rousing Samoan chantey, eager brown arms hauled at the mains'l. Lusty voices threw the rhythm into the air, filling the night with thunder. Up came the anchor from its bed of coral where it had rested for so many weeks. Judd and Ken watched the mains'l set. Now the wind was hauling out of the south. Matu, at the wheel, sniffed at the breeze and put the wheel down. The *Island Queen* moved slowly to the trickle of the ebb, turned south on a wide curve, and made toward the passage in the reef.

The ebb was gathering volume, running to meet the northerly current and setting up a stiff cross-sea. It needed a steady hand and a stout heart to take such a ship through such a narrow passage. But Matu knew what he was about. He lined up the brig dead-center for the opening. The ebb caught her in its flow. Like an arrow speeding to its mark she swept through the passage, lumbered through the cross-sea, cleared the reef, and pointed her nose westward.

The breeze stiffened. With every rag of canvas drawing the *Island Queen* rose to the long-rolling swells of the Pacific. A flock of gulls with eager cry followed her seaward. The two boys stood by the taffrail looking astern at the vanishing island. Now it was dropping farther and farther away down the reverse slope of a curve of water, as if to hide itself forever from the knowledge and concern of men.

A momentary depression settled upon Ken's spirit. His heart felt heavy, for it seemed that something fine and bright for him had vanished with Vana Vana. Ahead, there were only long vistas of books, a job waiting in a Museum, monographs to be written about people dead these thousand years—work he loved— but it was hard to leave that burial cave unexplored.

Judd saw him, and laughed. "Don't look so blooming glum! Anybody'd think we were never coming back here again!"

The other brightened. "We *are* coming back, Judd. It may be a year or two—but we'll sell the schooner and bank the money; and then one of these days . . ."

"Yes," the boy agreed, "one of these days. . . . Vana Vana wait for us." He was straining to watch the vanishing atoll, to see the last dark edge of wind-whipped palms. And in his eyes were morning, youth, and high adventure.

## CHAPTER XIV   A SHIP SAILS HOME

Four days later a cry from the lookout brought them all on deck with a bound.

"Ship ho! Starboard quarter!"

Through the glasses Judd could make out the sturdy lines of a cruiser, low-slung and moving swiftly along the horizon. As she drew nearer he saw the Union Jack fluttering at her peak. The *Island Queen* ran up her signals and backed her mainyards. The wind spilled from the brig's sails and she slowed to a reluctant halt, rocking in the long swells. The Samoans lined the rail, bursting with excitement. The cruiser, belching black smoke from her gray funnels, bore down upon the waiting brig.

"What ship is it?" Ken was asking eagerly.

Judd's hands trembled as he focused the glasses. "Can't quite make her out. . . . The B-L-A—the *Black Watch*," he decided finally. "I'll bet she's the cruiser that makes a biannual run through the islands of the British mandate. If she is, it's a stroke of luck for us. Her commander can take over our prisoners and the specie." He turned to the waiting Samoans and gave them the order to lower away the lifeboat. Then he hurried below to put on his shabby white jacket—the jacket that hadn't been on his back since the night he fled from Sing Fat's. A century ago all that seemed now. When he had slicked down his hair and shoved into his pocket the written and signed log of the cruise of the *Island Queen*, he was ready. Ken joined him.

The cruiser had stopped her engines. With four Samoans pulling on the oars, the brig's lifeboat skimmed across the waves, and Judd and Ken in the stern sheets tried vainly to conceal their excitement. They could see the cruiser's commander, and her

junior officers waiting by the ladder to receive their
visitors. And there were rows of "Limeys" lining the
rail. The sun flashed smartly on brightwork and
polished steel. This trim cruiser, shining with all the
devices of man's ingenuity for destruction, shattered
the peace and morning stillness of the Pacific. Here
was civilization. They had almost forgotten its
mechanized perfection.

A few moments more and the boys were introduc-
ing themselves to Commander Burne-Callander. The
man's eyes sparked with interest as he gripped their
hands and looked over these sunburned Americans in
their ragged patched clothes. Judd and Ken felt grimy
indeed as they observed their host's spotless white uni-
form with the gold braid of his rank glistening on his
shoulder straps. But the commander's quiet cordiality
put them at their ease.

As the man shook Judd's hand his first surprising
words were: "I would have recognized you anywhere, young man. But we'll get around to that later.
Come up to my quarters and tell me what this is all
about."

Judd had no time to ponder the strangeness of the
remark as the commander led them up to his cabin
off the bridge. Burne-Callander seated the boys comfortably, installed himself in a heavy chair behind a

desk, and looked at them with questioning eyes. Two young junior officers flanked their chief on either hand, and it was obvious that they had difficulty in concealing their curiosity.

"Well, young man?"

As Judd's story unfolded Burne-Callander's smile widened with good nature.

"I will be glad to take your prisoners off your hands," he said at length. "I'm on my way to Australia from New Guinea and the Commonwealth will be glad to settle accounts with Bergstrom. I know who he is. He passes himself off for a Swede, but he's really a German—was interned as a spy during the war. If I'm not mistaken he spent a number of years in the Melbourne 'pen.'"

"How about Red Malloy?" Judd asked. "Do you know him?"

"Who doesn't—in this part of the globe?" The commander wagged his head. "He's a bad customer. Last I heard of him he was in the jug in Port Moresby. I'd no idea he was on the loose again. I'll return to your ship with you and take over custody of these gentlemen; and oh, yes—the gold! I'd almost forgotten that." He pressed a bell, spoke into a telephone on his desk to give the necessary orders.

When they reached the *Island Queen* once more,

Judd took the commander below and handed over to him the written and signed story of the whole strange adventure.

"I translated this into Samoan, and it has been witnessed by each of the men," the boy explained. "And here is Matu's statement concerning the death of Karl Kassel."

"You declare these documents to be honest statements of all that has occurred?"

"I do."

"I find everything in perfect order, young man," Burne-Callander returned. "And now if you please—your prisoners."

Bergstrom and Red Malloy were led into the main cabin. The Swede, unshaved and unkempt, tried to make a show of unconcern as he stood before the immaculate Britisher. Malloy remained with lowered head, his lips twitching soundlessly. The commander threw a sharp glance at the latter, gave a startled exclamation, and jumped forward.

To the boys' utter amazement they saw Commander Burne-Callander grasp Red Malloy's hand and pump it up and down vigorously. Malloy broke into a laugh.

"Great work, Clydebank!" the commander cried. "I'd no idea *you* were in on this. I thought you were the villain of the piece!" He turned to the two mystified Americans with a laugh. "This prisoner of yours is Clydebank, one of the aces of the Colonial Intelligence Department, my friends. He's been on Bergstrom's trail for years. Great work, old chap!"

Axel Bergstrom's eyes seemed to burst into flame. An inarticulate sound strangled in his throat. He lunged forward, but Matu was too quick for him.

"Then—there isn't any Red Malloy?" Judd stammered.

Clydebank, alias Malloy, laughed good-naturedly. "Oh, yes, there is, my lad! Right in the jug at Port Moresby where he's been ever since he cooked up this cruise."

"And—and you——"

Malloy laughed again. "I'd probably never have gotten away with this impersonating job if Kassel hadn't been shot by Tor Jansen. Kassel hadn't seen Malloy in twenty years and I was taking a long chance on that."

Judd had a swift mental picture of that morning when Red Malloy first stepped on the deck of the *Island Queen;* he remembered the relief that had stamped the man's expression. "But——" the boy began.

Clydebank chuckled. It was the old familiar

chuckle of Red Malloy, yet oddly different now; and his *h*s seemed to have returned to proper place. "I know you're fair bustin' with questions. . . ." He was relishing the suspense to the full.

"Go on, man!" Ken shouted.

"All right, but first let me have a draw on a real cheroot of the commander's. . . ." He appropriated the Englishman's cigar, inhaled deeply with an ecstatic expression of bliss. "Bli'me! That's something like! Good cigars His Majesty supplies you fellows with! Nothing like that in the Intelligence. But Ken, here, is about to bust, so—here's the way of it: Red Malloy, the *real* one I mean, was a no-account Limey. He was first mate on the *Antipodes*. That was before the Intelligence learned that he was in the pay of Germany. Karl Kassel was commander of the U-boat that torpedoed the *Antipodes*, and Malloy had tipped the Germans off that all that gold was aboard. Malloy was an expert seaman, whatever else his shortcomings; he salvaged instruments from the tramp before she sank in Vana Vana lagoon, and took bearings and soundings of her position."

"How—how did you find all that out?" Judd asked.

Clydebank chuckled. "We got it out of him in the Port Moresby jug. When he made his getaway from Vana Vana he planned to keep secret the whereabouts of the gold and go back for it himself. The eighteen men of the *Antipodes* were divided up in two life-boats. One boat was wiped out by savages in the New Hebrides. The other boat reached Auckland some fifty days later with only four men aboard, and one of those four alive; Red Malloy. He had enough wit left to pretend lunacy. He could give no information whatever. Later, when he was released from hospital, he claimed amnesia. But the Intelligence was suspicious and for twenty-four years they kept an eye on him. When they learned that he had bought diving equipment they began to shadow his movements and watch his mail. Eventually the trail led to Karl Kassel, in Australia. Malloy wasn't getting any richer and he couldn't finance a lengthy salvage expedition on his own. He put the proposition up to Kassel."

"But where did Bergstrom and Tor Jansen come in?" Judd asked.

"They were Germans both," Clydebank replied. "Kassel owned this brig but had no money. Bergstrom had no money either, but he was a friend of Tor Jansen—and Jansen had wealth behind him, in Germany. Much good it ever did him!"

"Wealth!" exclaimed Ken incredulously. "Who on earth was he?"

"He was the only son of the great *Feldmarschall*

Kurt von Schleydt. He was born a mute, and a physical misfit into the bargain. The field marshal couldn't have an only son like that in Imperial Germany, so he shipped him out to German Samoa as a child. Tor spent the rest of his thwarted life taking out on other people his hatred of his father. When the Intelligence got wind of Malloy's scheme, we clapped him into the jug and I took a chance on impersonating him. We're both the same build, age, and general color-scheme. I had this scar carved on my cheek bone because Malloy had one just like it."

"I knew that scar wasn't an old one!" Judd reminded him ruefully.

Clydebank grinned. "If Bergstrom had been as smart and nosey as you two lads I'd have been in the soup."

"And I knew you didn't know your lead and latitude from a lamp-post," Judd finished. "But where'd you learn how to dive?"

"One of the few things I did learn back in my navy days," the other answered. "I did more than a bit of it on a mine sweeper in the North Sea. But I'd never have put it over if Tor Jansen hadn't shot Kassel in one of his rages."

"Phew!" ejaculated Ken. "If that doesn't beat——"

"Say!" Judd cried, sitting up with a start. "I'd

almost forgotten." He turned to Commander Burne-Callander. "What did you mean, sir, when you said you would have recognized me anywhere?"

The Englishman smiled, with such friendliness that Judd's heart warmed. He put an arm across the boy's shoulders. "I knew you were the son of Dexter Anders the moment I laid eyes on you," he said.

"You—you knew my father?" the boy stammered.

The man nodded. "In France. He fought for England even before America went into the war. He was the first American to receive the *croix de guerre*. I remember the day Pétain pinned it on his chest: there were four of us together. Lord—how long ago all that seems. . . . But I remember that he looked just as you look now. I used to hear from him occasionally after the Armistice. I'm a bad correspondent myself, I'm ashamed to say. But I know your father planned great things for you. . . ." The man was looking at Judd keenly, weighing him, gauging his metal.

Judd gripped the commander's hand, his heart full. "He *did* plan great things for me! He wanted me to go up to the mainland to college. He wanted me to learn and—and grow. I'm not going to let him down, sir!"

The crushing pressure of the Englishman's hand was his only answer. Then the commander was over the side and into his waiting boat. Axel Bergstrom was shoved down the ladder; he cowered on the floor of the boat, his face hunched between his shoulders. Then forty boxes bound about with rusty iron were lowered into the waiting boat. The gold of the *Antipodes*.

The *Black Watch* belched smoke from her funnels while the *Island Queen* dipped her ensign and received an answering salute. Within an hour the cruiser was a mirage fading on the horizon. The two boys and "Red Malloy" stood by the rail looking after her.

It was Ken who said, "I hate to think it's all over. What next, Judd?"

Judd smiled forlornly. "We'll have to sail for New Zealand, make our report to the authorities, and turn over the *Island Queen*. Gee! but I hate to say good-by to this ship!" He laid his hand affectionately on the taffrail.

"Perhaps," Clydebank suggested, "you won't have to."

"What do you mean?" the boy demanded.

"I mean there's a standing reward of two thousand pounds for the return of the gold of the *Antipodes*. And I'm sure the Colonial Government will sell you the *Island Queen* for a small portion of that."

Ken let out a shout of delight. "With our own schooner, Judd, the world's our oyster!"

Judd shook his head ruefully. "You heard what Burne-Callander said: my dad wanted great things for me. I'm going up to the mainland. Four years of grind, indoors out of the sun! But I'll give everything I've got to it; and when it's over I'm going home."

"Home?"

The boy nodded. "Tahiti." From the pocket of his jacket he drew a crumpled piece of paper: a bank draft for fifty-eight thousand francs, signed by Wong Fu.

"What are you going to do with that—frame it?"

"Buy back Dad's plantation! A college education needn't be a drawback to a planter. I'll put that plantation on the map, develop it. . . . And Mata Afa will be there, Ken. And Tetua Nui and—oh! they're swell people. You could do a dozen books about them."

"You haven't forgotten our *marae*, our burial cave on Vana Vana, have you? And our pile of black-lip, and——"

"I haven't forgotten any of it, you old fossil-hunter. You'll make an ethnologist out of me yet! Vana Vana's our next trip together." He gripped his friend by both arms, and hung on, his heart full, while Clydebank grinned at them with wide good nature.

"And you, Malloy," Ken laughed, "don't ever expect us to call you Clydebank! I suppose the missus will be on the dock in Auckland waiting for you, and say, 'Fancy meetin' you 'ere, you sweep!' "

Clydebank chuckled. "Lord help me if the missus ever learns how I maligned her!"

"We won't give you away."

The *Island Queen* came about on a new tack, her sails swelled drum-tight to the racing breeze, while the sun caught and threw back from the sea a thousand dancing spearheads of light.